One

August 2015

Before her thirtieth birthday, Honey Fontaine knew her mother wanted her married off, preferably to one of her friend's sons. He would have to possess a degree in finance, business, or medicine, and already be on a six-figure salary. He should have his own home or be in a position to purchase one in Kensington and Chelsea, Westminster or Richmond. And he should drive nothing less than a Porsche or Mercedes. Honey often thought that her mother's teenage pregnancy had given her the highest hopes on earth. Well, she had two years to go before the big three—O entered her life, and marriage wasn't on her vision board.

Honey sat staring at her reflection in her bedroom mirror, running a hand through her long, dyed auburn hair. Her Halle Berry style, Fatty had called it. Both her parents had been teenagers when she was born twenty-eight years ago, only her father hadn't stayed around to find out what his daughter looked like. The fifteen-year-old Kishan McNeely, son of an Ethiopian mother and an Irish-American father, was flown

out to Boston by his parents to continue his education unin-
terrupted, and to avoid taking any responsibility for a child.
Her mother, who had been thirteen at the time of Honey's
birth, was handed over to social services by her parents.

Picking up the small pot of lip gloss, Honey scooped a
little onto a small thin brush before applying it to her lips. She
picked up her black eyeliner. With a steady hand, she pulled the
ultra-thin brush along the bottom of her eyes before putting
it down. The sudden gust entering her bedroom caused her to
turn as her mother appeared.

'Honey, where are you going? I thought you were coming
with me to Lisa's dinner party.'

'What, so you can continue with your arranged marriage
business? I'm not interested in Lisa's son, and I'm sure I'm not
his type.'

'You only have to show your face. Lisa was just saying the
other day that Kyle was asking about you—come for an hour
or so.'

'You know I'm going to the carnival, Tasha. I told you I'm
on the float this year and it's my first time!'

'You sound like a teenager with low intellect. You'll never
find husband material at a carnival.'

'I'm not looking for a husband, don't you notice? And
today I feel like a teenager, so I'm going to act like one.'

'It worries me that you pick up these lowly estates behaviour, it's so unattractive—'

'Tasha! Quit, I'm not listening. You're such a snob.'

'Snob? No, Honey. I just happen to be a mother who

6

Love
Again

Rasheda Ashanti
Malcolm

JACARANDA

TWENTY
in 2020

Black Writers, British Voices

This edition first published in Great Britain 2020
Jacaranda Books Art Music Ltd
27 Old Gloucester Street,
London WC1N 3AX
www.jacarandabooksartmusic.co.uk

A CIP catalogue record for this book is available from the British
Library

ISBN: 9781913090258
eISBN: 9781913090456

Cover Design: Rodney Dive
Typeset by: Kamillah Brandes

Printed and bound by CPI Group (UK) Ltd, Croydon, CR0 4YY

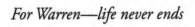
For Warren—life never ends

wants the best for my daughter, and I know what the best looks like, even if you don't.'

Two

August in London usually meant one big, exciting event. Notting Hill Carnival. Honey and her closest friends, Fatty and Zhara, bubbled with excitement as they squeezed into their carnival costumes, preparing for the float. The skimpy costumes left very little to the imagination, in true carnival style. Honey felt self-conscious in her red, green and gold bikini, beaded colourfully around the shape of her breasts.

'Hey Hon, you should stick some beads around your cookie area,' she pointed to Honey's privates. 'Be daring, it will go with the top.'

Honey shook her head in horror. 'No way, I feel like a hooker as it is—this is my daring. I feel completely naked.'

'It's your first time on a float—you're supposed to be near to naked. And when them hot guys start rubbing up on you, you gyrate back.' Fatty took her waist and hips slowly around a figure eight, and back again.

'Like this,' Zhara said, her high pert backside shaking as she twerked. She was at least 5'11 and her twerking was rigid and hilarious.

Fatty laughed, holding up a hand for a high five with

Zhara, both now screaming with laughter.

'I'm not having any strange man rubbing his self on me,' Honey huffed, giving Fatty a sharp look.

Fatty bounced Honey with a flick of her hip. 'Lighten up, Hon. Za is the Muslim here and she ain't complaining, she's twerking.'

'It's a bit of fun, Hon,' Zhara laughed lightly, placing a butterfly mask on her face. 'This is so my brothers don't recognise me as I give it all I got on the float.'

'Za, isn't this Haram? An insult to Islam?' Honey berated. 'And who's going to miss a tall girl like you, you can't hide.'

'You should try risk, Miss Goody-Goody.' Zhara danced around Honey, rubbing her generous breasts against her.

'Come,' Fatty grabbed her friends, 'let's go float.'

The loud music ringing out from the steel pans, the rowdy out of tune singing from the revellers and a few coconut rum punches finally influenced Honey to throw caution to the wind and enjoy herself. The barbecue chicken smell and smoke reminded her that her stomach was empty, but the soca music saturating the streets of Notting Hill pulled her arms, legs and backside into action. As the floats snaked their way around the crowded parade route, the London sky was clear and blue and the sun, like all the revellers, was bright and showing off.

'See how much fun you're having,' Fatty shouted in Honey's ear, taking her hands and twirling her around. Zhara joined them and began twerking. A group of young men circled them, cheering them on, as the three girls moved sensuously against each other.

'Every man's fucking fantasy,' Fatty laughed, pouring a splash from her cup over Honey's partially covered breast before running her tongue briefly across her chest. This brought great groans and cries for 'more' from the circling males and when Zhara bent over, placing both hands on the floor of the float to twerk, Fatty placing her hands on her bottom, all hell broke loose as revellers, male and female, started gyrating on each other to the sound of the pans.

'Hey, Fats, what's up?'

All three friends looked around and Honey found herself being swallowed by a pair of liquid amber coloured eyes, made sensuous by long curly lashes, and a smile that gave way to a dimple in his chin.

'Oh shit, Ash. Okay, okay. Honey Elizabeth Fontaine this is Ashley Elliott, or Ash if you like. Ash, this is Honey, the girl you were born to love. He's been wanting an introduction to you—'

'I've been waiting over three months,' Ashley cut in, his eyes unwavering as he continued to soak Honey up.

Honey looked bemused.

'I'll explain it to you later,' Fatty smiled cheekily.

'You'll explain it now!' Honey growled.

'Oh Hon, get off that high horse—this guy,' she pointed to an amused Ashley, 'is a successful businessman. He owns A One Studios and Club 21. He's rich!'

'And?' Honey quizzed, unimpressed.

'He, like so many others that I haven't told you about, has

the hots for you. He wanted an intro, that's all.'

'Fatty!' Honey exclaimed in a pained whisper.

'Hi Ash,' Zhara took a step closer to him. 'Long time no see.'

Ashley's eyes held Honey. Even when he was in conversation with Zhara.

'Za, shouldn't you be wearing a hijab? Your brothers know you're in the west?'

Zhara gave him a friendly shove. 'You know I live with my mum. So, you want to meet our Honey,' she teased.

'He wants to do more than meet her.' Fatty started dancing suggestively.

'You need my permission to introduce me to anyone,' Honey snapped. She didn't like the way he was looking at her and she liked it even less that she was near to naked under his gaze.

'Lighten up, Hon. The richest guy in West London wants an intro and you want to act like a snob!'

Ashley laughed, his gaze openly appreciative of Honey. 'I'm far from the richest guy, but now's not a good time,' he smiled, 'too much noise. A good time will come. I'll be seeing you, Miss Honey Elizabeth Fontaine.'

They watched as he climbed down from the float and disappeared into the crowd that lined the streets and the pavement.

'Fatty!' Honey turned on her. 'How could you do something so ridiculously childish?'

'It ain't childish, Hon. A man like Ashley Elliott wants an

intro to you... it's like a fucking miracle. He don't need to, girls throw themselves at his feet. He can have his pick of any but he seems to prefer his own company, or his little sister.'

Zhara sighed. 'I would marry Ashley.'

Fatty jumped up and down with laughter, swaying as the float went over a bump in the road. 'Don't be fucking crazy. Ash wouldn't give a girl like you a second glance, Za—he has a kind, more like Honey. He goes for classy chicks. You'd be left heart-broken.'

Honey frowned. 'And I won't? You want him to break my heart?'

Fatty grabbed her and started dancing; 'He wouldn't get close enough to break your fucking heart, Hon. You got some serious ice packs in your chest and I know Ash won't find it easy to get you. You're made of icy frost, Za of candy floss; she disintegrates when she's in love and she falls for fools all the time.'

The Carnival after party was taking place at Club 21. Honey, Fatty and Zhara jumped off the float on St Charles Road, taking the back route into Shepherds Bush where they made their way towards Fatty's home on the estate and changed out of the skimpy carnival costumes, donning light blue faded jeans and white fitted tank tops with white Nike trainers. Honey styled both her friends' hair, before turning the straightening tongs on her own, ironing out all her curls. They posed in the mirror, looking at themselves and each other, then took pictures.

'I wish I could lose some weight,' Fatty pulled in her

bulging stomach. 'You two look so slim and sexy.'

'Lots of men like fat girls,' Zhara empathised. 'You're sexy too,' she squeezed Fatty's breast.

'You need to eat more green foods and less of the white foods,' Honey told her.

'The two of you can suck my dick!' Fatty spat with good humour. 'Za looks like a spaghetti, Honey you look like a cucumber and me, I look like a melon.'

In the dark, smoky atmosphere vibrating with heavy bass music, the girls created a space for themselves just by Fatty's bold walk. They settled in the corner by a huge speaker box.

'Look,' Fatty pointed out to Honey, 'there's Ash on stage.' Honey saw his tall, lean figure dressed in denim, dreadlocks bouncing on his shoulder as he danced across the stage.

'What the hell is he doing?' Honey couldn't help her amusement.

'It's one of his clubs—he always gets the crowd wild.'

And he did, Honey observed. There were girls trying to climb on the stage, one successful who made a dash to throw her arms around him, only to be dragged away screaming by the security.

'What's so great about him?' Honey asked. She didn't like this kind of music. She didn't mind soca and reggae, rare groove, but this was something else.

'He owns this fucking club, Hon. He owns the most successful studio in West London, he can have any girl but he wants you... he's got it bad for you.'

'That doesn't make him great.'

'Those girls think so.'

'And they're experts in what?'

After two hours Honey was ready to go, but could see Fatty and Zhara were nowhere near. She eased through the crowd, signalling to Fatty that she was going outside. The fresh, cool air was welcoming and she walked to stand around the corner from the main door, leaning against the brick wall with her eyes closed. It had been a long day, starting at 5:15am with the finishing touches to their costumes, hairdressing appointment which ran over, manicure and pedicure. It was all crashing in now. She wanted her bed.

'You okay?'

Opening her eyes, she found she was swimming in a familiar pair of amber eyes. His lips were full with moodiness, unbelievably luscious and alluring. His dreadlocks just passed his shoulders, black and brown hair tangled into even shaped coils that hung untidily around his face. It was him, Ashley, and now she was this close to him a small bubble of interest popped. He was with some other guy who was tall, bleach blonde and thin with a tan, prettier than any girl she knew. He was dressed in skin tight jeans and tight pink tee shirt that clung to his slim, boyish, feminine body.

'This is my cousin, Dame,' Ashley responded to her quizzical look towards Dame.

'Why are you chilling on your own? Is it so boring inside?' Ashley asked.

She took her eyes reluctantly off Dame and viewed Ashley. 'I'm just going back inside, if you must know.'

'You pissed with me? Did I do something I don't know about?' Ashley pursued.

Honey started walking and Ashley and Dame followed closely. She found her way back to Fatty and Zhara, who it seemed hadn't stopped dancing for a second as their sweat soaked faces and white tee shirts showed.

'Hey Hon, you found Ash,' Fatty shouted above the music, her arm frantically moving around her head, a bottle of Smirnoff on its way to her mouth.

'I wasn't looking for anyone,' Honey clarified.

'I found her,' Ashley told Fatty.

Dame took Honey's hand. 'Ash has been fantasizing about you for so long, it's so good to finally meet you.' His smile was pretentious but friendly. Honey warmed to him, she couldn't help it.

Ashley swiftly removed her hand from Dame's and gently steered her to look at him. 'Wanna drink?' he leaned and whispered in her ear.

She shook her head, the feel of his lips too close for comfort.

'Wanna dance with me?'

'Hell no!'

'I didn't ask you to bed, I asked for a dance.' He held out a hand.

'No thanks,' she presented a brief plastic smile.

'Can I see you home?'

'Hell no.'

'You know any other word?'

Honey could see she was on her own with this. Fatty and Zhara were out crazy on the music, the crowd was still a mass and nobody looked like they were going anywhere too soon.

'Look,' she told him, 'Fatty shouldn't have done what she did. I really don't know you. Can you leave me alone?'

Ashley looked taken aback, but nodded. 'Okay. If you dance with me, I'll leave you alone.'

Before she could change her mind, she grabbed his hand, pulling him towards the dance floor. 'Okay, I'll dance with you but after this, you leave me alone.'

Then they just had to put on a Boyz to Men oldies; *End of the Road*. Ashley pulled her in close, too close, as he moved deliciously against her. Honey was shocked. Surprised. She had not expected to feel the rush she did. His movements were sensuous and his smell was alluring and spicy. When the music stopped, he didn't let her go, and she didn't move from out of his arms as quick as she would have liked. Before she knew it, he was moving against her again and, to her horror, she felt her stomach reaching for her heart. As the next song dissipated, she withdrew from his arms, smiled robotically and walked very quickly over to Fatty and Zhara, only to find them entwined in the arms of some guys she had never seen before.

Ashley was by her side again, two bottles in his hand. She was about to refuse his offer until she saw hers was a pineapple juice and it still had its lid intact. Feeling thirsty and safe in the fact he couldn't have spiked it, she reluctantly took the bottle.

'What's wrong? You don't like the way I dance?' he asked, his lips lightly touching her ear. She moved away so she could look in his face. It was too dark to see much of his features but she remembered the colour of his eyes. Amber.

'Did you expect me to stay in your arms all night?' She shouted above the music.

'That would have been nice,' his lips were back on her ear.

'You need to know now that you're not my type,' she delivered.

'What's your type?'

'None of your business. Do you mind not speaking any more? Just I don't want your spit in my ear and I don't want to keep shouting.'

She had shocked him, she could see it. She hoped she had disturbed his sense of confidence, but he recovered a smile and nodded knowingly as though he knew her, which only served to annoy her more.

She looked around at the noisy crowd, and as her eyes drifted from face to face, she became startled by a pair of eyes, waiting like nets to catch her. They were dark with feelings, pleading and sorrowful. Honey looked away, suddenly uncomfortable at being an audience to such sadness on a stranger.

Fatty appeared beside them, breathless with sweat running down the sides of her face.

'Wow, that brother can dance,' she beamed at Honey. 'What's wrong with your face, Ash giving you stress?' She laughed, nudging Ashley.

'Are you ready?' Honey asked Fatty point blank.

'No!' Fatty retorted, 'the night is young just free up a bit, Hon.'

She felt Ashley's hand on her elbow. 'Come,' he said signalling with his head, 'I'll drop you home.'

Honey snatched her elbow away.

'Oh, let him Hon. It will be safe and save you a taxi fare going on your own like this... unless you want to wait until me and Za are ready.'

That could mean until the club closed. Honey didn't want that. She didn't want Ashley Elliott taking her home either. But as Fatty pointed out, it would save her a taxi fare and she was already over her budget for the month, which she would have to explain to her mother when she asked for yet another loan. She looked at her watch; it was 2am.

'He's harmless Hon... you can manage him,' Fatty whispered.

And Honey felt she could. Somehow, she knew she would be safe with Ashley Elliott. She allowed him to hold her hand as he made way through the throbbing crowd, stopping briefly to respond to congratulatory handshakes and fist and shoulder knocks. Outside, the early morning London air was crisp and carried no hint of the scorching sun that had serenaded them on the float the previous day.

'Let's go for a drive,' he suggested, his eyes twinkling.

'You promised to give me a lift home, and that's all I'll be grateful for, a lift to my door, thank you.'

Ashley held the car door open for her to get in, and as she sat down the seat belt automatically wrapped around her like an arm. She was impressed, but stifled it. They drove slowly out of the private car park and Honey saw her again. *Those eyes.* The same girl who had been watching them inside. She smiled as they passed and Honey wasn't sure who at, she just knew she had never known a smile to spread such sadness across a face.

He drove his shiny BMW at high speed on A40 towards Uxbridge, before doing an illegal U turn and heading back towards Ealing. Honey noted that her mother would at least approve of his car.

'You better hope no cameras snapped you or you'll be getting a sixty-five pound fine in the post.'

'We'll split the cost.' He winked before returning his eyes to the road.

'I'm not the one driving.' She stifled a yawn she created just for him.

Finally he reduced his speed and pulled up outside a 24-hour bagel shop on Ealing Common, coming back with two steaming chicken bagels, and cups of hot chocolate. 'Our first breakfast together,' he smiled in that cheeky way that made her heart walk a little faster. 'You must be hungry after using up all those calories on the float; I didn't notice you eating all day. You shake it pretty good though,' he laughed at the frown that crossed her face.

As they sat eating in silence, she couldn't help liking him. *'Like'*, she told herself. She was involuntarily impressed by his action, buying her early morning breakfast. It showed thoughtfulness she thought.

She directed him to stop a few doors away from her house, in a cul-de-sac of impressive looking semi-detached Victorian houses, all with large windows and perfectly framed land-scape. Across the road, separating a large green common, was a stream. The early morning August sun was making its way through the white clouds. She knew from experience that the hazy white mist settling on the stream was a sure sign of a hot summer's day. She didn't want to sleep.

'It's 3:20am. Your folks gonna kick up?'. His cheeky grin was back.

'I'm not a child.'

'I can see that.' He placed a half smoked spliff between his lips.

She removed it and put it back in the ashtray. 'Don't smoke in front of me. I value my health.'

Ashley laughed. 'I respect that.'

'I doubt that.'

He looked at her seriously for the first time. 'You think you can ease up a bit so I can get to show you how much I like you, and you can get to know me and maybe even like me?'

'I'm not interested.'

'Why? You have someone?'

'Well, whether I do or not, it's not your concern.'

'You know, the reason I asked Fatty for an introduction to you is because I was scared to ask myself. I see I should have been a lot more scared. You're even more wonderful than I thought' he chuckled warmly.

Honey looked at him and wished she could believe him.

Three

September 2015

Ashley had finally met Honey Fontaine. He was pleased with himself, despite her frost. It was early evening and he still hadn't caught up with any significant sleep after carnival Monday, and all the events his club had since then. His sleep was frequently interrupted by Honey creeping into his head, and he kept reliving her disapproving gestures, her frowns and negative response to him, removing his spliff from his mouth like she had the authority. Thinking about her made him smile, laugh even. Clearly Honey was confident, and Fatty's words about other men's admiration for her did not go amiss. She was a challenge, but he wasn't disappointed.

Ashley was sitting in the small office adjacent to the chill room, going over the final proofs of the flyers for their forthcoming, half term, family day in the park, in association with Hammersmith and Fulham Council. His selected few, Dame and Richie, were with him, sitting around the table viewing the proofs critically.

'I'm not too sure about that green,' Richie complained,

tapping impatient fingers on the proofs. 'It reminds me too much of the green Dame threw up after eating that Indian food with the spinach.'

'Go fuck yourself,' Dame said quite politely, flicking non-existent hair out of his face.

'Okay ladies, no cat fights now,' Ashley spoke with distraction as he viewed the proofs. 'Maybe we should have the green a little lighter and the red a little darker... yes, I think that would do it.'

Just then his phone rang. He didn't recognise the number but answered it anyway.

'Talk to me,' he said.

'Hi Ash, it's me—'

'Fatty! Who's with you?'

'No, Hon isn't with me. But she just called to say she thinks she dropped her pearl earring in your car... her Mum bought it so she'd like you to look and I can come pick it up or you can drop it to me.'

'Tell her to call me and ask me herself.'

Fatty heaved a sigh. 'Ash, she—'

'Tell her if she wants it, she calls me and I'll drop it off, I know where she lives. And tell her no blocked number.'

When his phone rang a few minutes later and he saw the unfamiliar number he smiled.

'Talk to me.'

'Ashley Elliott...' His heart leapt. He stood up and walked to the other side of the room where the leather sofas were.

'Miss Fontaine,' he found himself smiling into the phone.

'Not quite sure why you wanted me to make this request myself, but can you see if I dropped my earring in your car? It's a white pearl stud. My mother gave it to me and she'll go ballistic if she knows I've lost it. Can you have a look and meet me with it, ASAP?'

The thought of seeing her warmed him. 'Cool. I'll pick you up at the corner of your cul-de-sac in about half an hour.'

'Who's that?' Richie enquired as Ashley took his car keys off the table.

'Honey Fontaine.' He smiled with a weird look in his eyes.

'Oh, Fatty's snobby friend. You know she don't like me? She don't talk to me; she hardly talks to anyone.'

'Does she have to?' Ashley threw over his shoulder as he walked out the door, storing her number in his phone.

She was standing at the entrance of the cul-de-sac in a fitted denim dress that stopped on her thighs, feet snug in gestapo boots hugging her slender legs. He pressed the button and the window slid down. She was unsmiling but looked beautiful, her hair piled in a bun.

'Hi.' His smile was slow and warm.

'Did you find my earring?'

'Is that how you greet people? No warmth, no smile. Hi?'

She folded her arms. 'Hi, did you find my earring please?'

He held out a folded tissue. 'Here.' She took the tissue and opened it, her face breaking into a relieved smile.

'Wow, you can smile,' Ashley acted surprised.

Honey looked less hostile. 'I was worried I'd lost it, thank you.'

'Want to come for a drive? Anywhere you want.'

She shook her head. 'No, I have work tomorrow and I'm still recovering from carnival—I've only had about five or six hours sleep per night.'

'Lucky you, I haven't slept yet. You sure you won't come for a drive?'

'Quite sure. Not with a sleep deprived driver. Bye.' She turned and walked away.

'I'll be seeing you.'

'Not if I see you first,' she threw over her shoulder.

'Your low self-esteem is a turn on,' he called out, and thought he saw the trace of a smile when she briefly threw him a look.

*

Ashley Elliott was a middle child, and he was used to what people said about middle children. Only Ashley had the first child syndrome after he was forced to fill his older brothers' shoes. Nathan had left home two weeks after their father did, breaking his mother's heart twice in one month. His mother had been eight months pregnant and forty-five years old. Ashley was ten years old and became her rock.

The first time he noticed something different about his mother was after the birth of his sister; her sadness was constant and she refused to leave the house. She went out just once and that was to register the baby. She didn't even have a name in her head when they sat in Hammersmith Registry of

Birth and Death. He was the one who blurted out "Marley," when the registrar became impatient with his silent mother. It was the only name he could think of and, because Bob Marley was his hero, he thought it very fitting.

Ashley was left to fend for the family: to put the weekly wash in the machine, cook, look after Marley and shop. He wanted dearly to bring the smile back to his mother's face, the smile he remembered before Marley. There was a time when every weekend she used to teach him to cook and clean a house, and in the evenings she'd sit and listen to him play the piano. He would often play *Many Rivers to Cross*. She told him it was the only song she could dream to. That was before his father left, walked out on her for another woman twenty-two years his junior.

It was two years before his mother started going out again, and that was just to church, which she became fanatical about. She would not miss morning or evening service if it killed her, ignoring the care of Marley. She had re-discovered God and the church became her life. But even with God as the new man in her life, Ashley still heard her crying at nights and calling his father's name out in prayer. How he hated the man.

Then when Marley was two years old, after numerous attempts on her own life, his mother was diagnosed as schizophrenic with associated bi-polar disorder. Social Services entered his life, placing him and Marley with their Auntie Dawn during his mother's lows. Ashley had hated Nathan too, for leaving them when they most needed him. But when Nathan had come back nine years later, a day after Ashley's nineteenth birthday, he brought wealth with him. Ashley remembered so well the day. He hardly recognised his brother who was now thirty years old and had a beard. By then Ashley and Marley were living with their mother again because she had become stable and was taking her medication.

Nathan had done well in Chicago and had made money. He worked in the music industry and came with suitcases filled with clothes for his mother and siblings. Best of all, he bought a spacious two bedroom flat in a gated community in Kensington, West London. Before returning to America six months later, he left Ashley in charge of it.

'You're nineteen now, but you've got an old head on young shoulders,' Nathan had told him, handing him the keys to the flat. 'I'm leaving you in charge. I don't want you using it for no gang bangs or all-night parties. If the caretaker tells me any of that stuff is going on, I'll fly straight back for the keys—are you hearing me?' Nathan looked dead serious, like his father used to when he wanted his full attention.

Ashley was ecstatic. 'I won't let you down, blood. I'm going to make something of my life, just you wait and see.'

Nathan had grabbed the back of his neck playfully. 'My little bruv, all grown up!' He laughed. 'The flat can be your space, somewhere to get away from it all for a few days. Maybe one day when you're ready, you can come join me in Chicago. There's more opportunity over there. You think about it.'

Ashley had been excited but also worried about leaving his mother and Marley.

'Yeah, when Marley gets a bit older and can keep an eye on

Moms. She's happy enough now but she could fall in a mood in seconds, and it could last for months.'

'It's good how you look after Moms and how you take care of Marley. I'm going to send more money every month.' Nathan at least had the decorum to look and feel guilty. 'I had to harden my heart to walk out on you all, but I couldn't stay. I'm real proud of the way you've turned out, you did a whole lot better than me and Dad.'

Ashley's face hardened at the mention of his father.

'I see him sometimes,' Nathan whispered. 'Dad. I see him now and again. He's in Chicago with some new woman called Lola, although it looks to me like she's just milking him.'

Ashley was gob-smacked. From what Nathan was saying it seemed as if he was in regular contact with the man who abandoned them, who was responsible for their mother losing herself.

'Just forgive him, Ash. He's not a bad man, he just fell out of love with our Moms and in love with someone else. And there's good reasons for that. There's always two sides to a story; when I think you're ready I'll tell you Dad's side.'

'I don't need to hear it. I don't ever want to see him again.'

Four

September 2015

'The next time you decide you're going to stay out all night, I'd be very grateful if you let me know so that I don't spend the whole night worrying that you've been shot, raped, or strangled!' Natasha told her daughter over dinner, a week after Carnival had ended.

'Sorry, Tasha, you remember what Carnival is like, the time just ran away.' Honey had used her mother's first name since childhood and Natasha had long stopped trying to get her to change. Her being thirteen years old when she had Honey, and living with a foster family and a young baby after being rejected by angry parents, meant Honey grew up calling her *Tasha*, just like she heard everyone else did.

'Was he nice?' Her father asked, spooning broccoli onto his plate as a smile tugged the corners of his mouth. He was handsome, with a head full of distinguishing silver hair and skin tanned by sun beds. His green eyes were pale and soft and his smile kind and fatherly.

'I wish you wouldn't make a joke of this, Aaron, I was

frantic,' Natasha's forehead developed two lines for an instant. At forty-one she was still youthful and often mistaken for Honey's sister. Natasha was a woman who loved taking care of herself. Her hair, nails, body and face all had appointments. She knew she was fortunate to have found Aaron, she had been given a second chance at life and had made good of it. That was what she now wanted for her child.

'But I told you there was no need to worry. Honey's sensible and, more than that, she's old enough,' Aaron quipped, his head nodding meaningfully.

'Many sensible girls end up raped, strangled or shot and buried in some shallow grave,' Natasha snapped, annoyed that her husband wasn't taking this as seriously as she was, and as usual was trying to play peacekeeper.

'I'm sorry, Tasha,' Honey smiled sweetly, 'I should've called. What can I say to make it up?'

'You can start by saying it won't happen again.' Natasha flapped her napkin before placing it on her lap.

'It won't happen again,' Honey surrendered. 'It was just that the carnival after party was kicking.'

'Kicking? Don't use language like that around me, it's annoying, and you're not a teen. Where was this until those ungodly hours?' Natasha asked before biting into the corn on the cob, its juices spraying onto the table cloth. She mopped at it with her napkin.

'Club 21, I went with Fatty.'

Natasha's hand flew to her head. 'Honey, I have nothing against Vannese, but her mother is an alcoholic and a drug addict. There's even talk of her prostituting herself, it's no secret,' she warned solemnly.

Honey sighed. 'It's not Fatty's fault, we can't help who our mothers are.'

Natasha raised her well-shaped eyebrows. 'Is that a knock at me?'

'No, Tasha. Fatty's mum has real issues. She's searching for what most women want, love, and when she doesn't find it, she turns back to the drugs and alcohol.'

Natasha raised her brows again. 'Is that what she has her poor daughter believing? Poor Vanesse. I like her, but she's not really the right company for you.'

'There you go again, thinking you can choose my boyfriends and my friends. Fatty is my bestie.'

Natasha placed the corn back on her plate and wiped each finger with the napkin. 'I'm just pointing out a fact known to everyone; her mother is a drunk, a drug addict and a prostitute!'

'Maybe, but her daughter isn't! And I'm old enough to choose my friends, in case you forgot.'

Aaron, who was used to the battles between his wife and daughter, thought it time to step in. He cleared his throat. 'I'd still like to meet him,' he said to Honey, changing the conversation.

'Meet who?' Natasha queried.

'The gentleman who's stolen Honey's heart and kept her out all night.'

Honey amazed herself by blushing and touching her chest

30

to ensure her heart was still in place. She laughed inwardly at such a childish action.

'Do we know his family?' Natasha's curiosity was raised. She was cautious in her approach. 'Now's not the time to be distracted, Honey. You haven't got a permanent contract yet. Don't you know any young men at work?'

Honey huffed. 'Yes, but they're boring, already committed, or gay.'

Natasha heaved inwardly. 'If you're thinking of getting serious with anyone, I think we have a right to know. That's how things are done in this family.'

'I'm not serious, I just met him...' *Maybe she should let her mother believe she was heading for love.* 'It's early days, Tasha. I'll let you know about any developments.' Honey concealed the urge to smile by producing a small cough. She knew her mother was trying to screen her disapproval.

'It's your life but please, Honey, don't give yourself to anyone who won't love and respect you. Make sure he deserves you.'

'I will.'

'Mrs Muller says her son, Sam, has been working in America and is coming back to England. He's got a good job lined up in the City, and is looking to settle down. I told Mrs Muller that we'd come to his welcome lunch.'

'The last time I checked, we don't arrange marriages in our culture. Are you serious?' Honey fumed.

The frown didn't shift from Natasha's face. 'Don't you want the best? You won't find husband material in the places you—'

Honey's frustration showed. 'Which century are you living in, Tasha?'

Natasha bit into a carrot. 'The last I checked, marriage was still very much current and you're nearly twenty-nine. Now I'm not trying to choose your friends but Sam Muller is a good catch and you'll at least meet him, there's no harm in that. Let's say no more on the matter.'

Aaron cleared his throat noisily. He knew his wife had yet to cut the invisible umbilical cord.

'Honey is quite right, Natasha. She's old and ugly enough to choose her friends. I trust my daughter's judgement and if she has someone... I'd like to meet him.'

Honey smiled. 'You know, Daddy, I think I might just believe in love at first sight, it's happened all so quickly. I'll let you know when he can come to dinner.'

Natasha choked before her wine glass could touch her lips.

Five

'Bella,' Fatty kicked at the crumpled mass of duvet on the living room floor. 'Look at the fucking state of the room. Get up you sorry arse piece of shit.'

The crumpled mass moved and suddenly there was a dishevelled, distorted shape of a human being, her face puffy, red and oblivious, her hair dyed black, straggly and greasy.

'Bella, get the fuck up. Go wash yourself and eat something.'

'Fatty, why you shouting, you're hurting my fucking head. That's no way to talk to your fucking mother!'

Fatty pulled the duvet completely off. 'You've never been a mother so don't ever mention that word to me. Now get up coz I've got Honey coming over and I don't want her to see you like this again.'

Honey was her best friend and had everything she ever wanted. Fatty was aware of their differences, aware that no matter how hard she tried she would never have what Honey had: a mother and father who loved her. Fatty wondered for many years how she and Honey started life with teenage mums, yet Honey's mother came up smelling of roses.

Vanesse Derby, or Fatty to her friends, lived with her mother in a two-bedroom West London council flat on the Eagleton estate, where gangs made their presence known in the graffiti that occupied any blank walls, stairways and lifts. She had always lived there. Eighth floor was hell to get to between the urine-soaked lifts and the urine-soaked stairways when the lifts were broken. Her mother was the estate's drunk. Her childhood still had the power to make her physically sick if she thought too long or too hard about it.

Fatty was five years old before she even knew her name was Vanesse and not Fatty. She remembered some of the dads her mother brought home: Tony, Lee, Jim, Spencer, Tom, Joe, Ali, Mohammed, Neville, Sean and many more. That was her experience of fathers. She knew something was missing, she just didn't know what until she met Honey.

✻

Honey sat watching Fatty apply lipstick to her pouting lips. She made an 'ummm' sound, ensuring that the lipstick spread equally. Her small, white walled bedroom could easily have been mistaken for a beauty boutique with the variety of makeup and perfumes that adorned every inch of the white dresser.

'That's a nice colour,' Honey told her. 'Is it new? Fenty,' she read the label on the tube. 'Rihanna's brand. Let's see if it suits me.'

Fatty grabbed the lipstick out of her hand. 'It's not cheap. I'll share my mango with you because I can get three for a fiver, but for every layer of that lipstick you put on, I have to charge you £2.'

'You kidding me? Keep your freaking lipstick.'

'Anyway, Ash says he likes it that you're so natural. He says you're a natural beauty,' Fatty sang.

'Are you still talking to him?' Honey couldn't stop the scorn spreading itself across her face or the flutter of her heart at the mention of his name.

'One thing you gotta know about Ash, he's persistent. There's a sweetness to him, Hon, he just hides it really well. Maybe a little sugar from Honey is all he needs,' Fatty laughed indulgently at her own joke.

'He doesn't interest me. He's full of ego.' Honey sounded annoyed.

'You don't know him; you hardly know anyone. Tasha had you stuck in private school, then college, then uni. You missed out on so much living by her laws, Hon. Ash is far from egotistical.'

Honey turned to view her friend. 'And I should live by your laws where you just introduce me to strangers?'

Fatty laughed. 'You're never going to forgive me for that, are you?'

'Hell no.'

'That's okay, as long as you love me.'

That coaxed a smile from Honey's irritable lips. 'You are

something else, Fats. Anyway, Ashley might just be useful. Tasha's back wanting to introduce me to a potential husband—you know how she is—so I pretended I met someone at the Carnival. Daddy wants to meet him and of course it's killing her. I kind of want to keep her wondering.'

Fatty looked dubious. 'How would that work?'

'I'd pretend to have a relationship with Ashley. That way Tasha will ease off her wedding plans for me, hopefully.'

'I'm not sure if Ash would go along with something like that... he's a proud man. What would be in it for him?'

'Can't he just do us a favour for nothing?'

Fatty burst into fits of laughter. 'What world are you living in, girl. There's no such thing as something for nothing.' She winked at Honey in the mirror. She whipped out a wet wipe from its packet and cleaned her hands before picking up an eyebrow pencil.

'Although, I've never seen him want to meet a girl as badly as he did you. I couldn't believe it, all the pestering for months to get an intro. I mean, Ash can get any girl like that,' she clicked her fingers. 'But he's always been picky, even more so since Bethany, his ex. I guess you've got the It factor, girl! You're not fazed by him. I think he finds it a turn on.'

Honey thought more seriously about her plan. She appreciated the fact that Natasha wanted the best for her. But Honey felt she had to halt these lunches and dinners Tasha insisted on, all in aid of meeting some-one's well-to-do son who needed a wife.

'So, this ex, where is she now?' Honey tried to sound

casual.

'Still around, although not in Ash's life. He wouldn't touch her with a barge pole. She slept with one of his business buddies—big story back then. He's unforgiving about that, what man ain't?'

'I'm going to ask him to pretend to be in love with me.'

Fatty swung around from the mirror to view Honey. 'For real?'

'Yes. Tasha won't be able to find fault with his income, and you know that's the number one requirement on her list for potential husbands.'

'Crazy bitch! He might just do it to get close to you, and by close, I mean inside.'

Honey laughed. 'He could never seriously get a girl like me.'

Fatty jumped on the bed and lay down beside her. 'Love the chat girlfriend but don't let your guard down. Guys like Ash are easy to fall in love with.'

'I don't doubt that, but he's only just met Honey Elizabeth Fontaine.'

Fatty got up laughing and smoothed down her dress. She turned at different angles to look at herself in the mirror. 'You talk like you got something between your legs sweeter than any other woman.' She viewed her backside in the mirror. 'I wash my hands of this and I sure as hell ain't going to take no blame when the shit hits. How do I look? You think I'm too fat to wear a dress like this?'

Honey turned on her back and smiled at her friend. Fatty

was voluptuous, curvaceous, a good size sixteen with olive brown skin and short black curly hair, which she dyed a variety of auburn or red, even blue when she felt like it. She pointed the remote at the television and switched it on.

'You're beautiful, Fatty.'

Fatty sat on the bed beside her friend. 'I so love you. But man do I wish I had your wash bowl stomach.' She slapped Honey's stomach playfully.

Honey laughed. 'It's board... washboard not bowl.'

'Whatever. I wish I knew what my father looks like, you know—who I get my shape from, my backside, these thick thighs, my eyes, nose and mouth. It's not Bella. I obviously take more of the Black side than Bella's Italian blood. She hasn't a clue who my father is, but says if she ever saw him again, she would know him. She's never seen him again.' Fatty sighed as Honey gave her arm a comforting pat.

Their attention was taken by the advert that flashed across the television screen. Images of starving African women with long, thin bodies and babies cradled in bony arms sucking from stretched out breasts.

'I hate when they show those images of poor, starving women in Africa,' Honey said sadly. 'It's belittling. It makes me feel so hopeless.'

'I'd give anything to be that thin,' Fatty piped.

Honey looked at her in dismay. 'Oh Fatty, that is so not funny.'

Fatty laughed, as she always did at Honey's disapproval. 'I wasn't trying to be funny; I'd love to be that thin... it ain't far off what them supermodels look like.'

Honey rolled her eyes, stuttering at what to say to such a thing when a knock at the door brought a hush to the room.

'What!' Fatty yelled. The door opened and her dishevelled mother swayed in.

'I just took a phone call for you,' she told Fatty. 'Some girl says to tell you she's having another baby for Sonny, and that you know who she is.'

Fatty didn't move. She stared ahead unblinking. She knew who the call was from. Stacey, one of Sonny's bitches who was unfortunate enough to have given him two babies in as many years. Now she was on her third and wanted Fatty to know.

'I think you should find a decent man,' Bella slurred. 'That Sonny don't respect you. You should hear the things the girl was—'

'What would you know about respect? I never asked for your opinion. Close the door on your way out!' Fatty pointed.

'I'm speaking the truth,' Bella slurred, looking at Honey. 'Tell her Honey. Tell her to listen—'

'Just get the fuck out, you drunk! When everyone knows your mother gives a good blow job for two bits of brown or some white, she's got no fucking say! Get out!'

Bella turned slowly, head held down, and walked out.

Honey's silence spoke volumes, but Fatty was too mad to care. 'Don't say a word, Honey, not one fucking word. She fucking deserved that!'

'You know she didn't. She's a junkie, but she's your mum and she cares about you.'

'She only cares about her drugs and her booze... nothing else.'

'Why do you keep letting Sonny get away with cheating on you? Why don't you leave him?'

'Because I refuse to jump from man to man like my fucking mother, okay! I want people to respect me, even though I'm the daughter of a drug addicted whore. Anyway, that big belly man, Sonny, can keep buying me, because that's what he does. He buys me. And I hardly ever fuck him. See the Burberry luggage set? And that pair of LK Bennett shoes? And the Louis V handbag? He bought it all for me, claiming he really loves me. That's why I put up with him.'

'You gold-digger!' Honey giggled, 'Girl you got some front.'

Fatty raised her eyebrows seductively and patted her private area. 'So I've been told.'

'But did you hear your mum, Fatty? She does care.'

'It's a bit late to fucking care now. She should have fucking cared when I was seven years old and needed her drunk arse help!'

Six

Ashley was driving on the M6 returning from Birmingham, trying to reach London ahead of the torrential rain that threatened. His phone rang and he flinched at the crackling sound of the ear piece. The sound of Honey's sweet voice cast any shadows away. He couldn't account for her sudden desire to meet, or the mysterious proposal she hinted at, but he cleared his schedule without question. If Honey had changed her mind, he wanted to catch her before the fickle tides could change again.

As he pulled up at the mouth of the cul-de-sac, she was already there. Her white jumper and the pristine white pumps on her feet made her look like an advert for a washing powder or fresh smelling perfume. A wavy brown river of hair rested past her shoulders.

'Could you turn that music down? Can't you see the neighbours' curtains moving? They'll be calling the environmental people to close us down.' She was of course talking about what could only be called a sound system in a car, but he complied.

'I must remember to lower my music when driving this royal way, in case it lowers the house prices,' he teased.

'Very funny,' she smirked.

He licked his lips. 'So, did your parents kick up at the time you got in after carnival?'

'I'm a grown woman, they don't have a say.'

He laughed. She was grown alright. An image of her naked in his bed, her hair spread across his pillow, flashed before him.

'You want to go for a drive?'

'Yeah, let's go to Battersea Park. My uni friend has invited me to her birthday barbecue.'

'I thought you wanted to talk serious?'

'Yeah, and I will. Actually, this will be the first of the tests if you agree to my proposal.'

Ashley started the engine, still looking at her sideways, taking in her smile, the way she was so not in awe of him. He turned the car around and drove slowly until they met the main Uxbridge Road.

'I'm hot to know about this... test,' he glanced at her thick brown hair.

'I need a favour. Just hear me out, no rude insinuations or jokes.'

'I'm listening.'

'I need someone to act like my boyfriend. My mother has adopted the arranged marriage culture and is vigorously seeking a husband for me. I told her that I was already in love so now my dad wants to meet the guy... and of course he doesn't exist yet, so I have to create him. That's where you come in.'

They hit heavy traffic just as they got over Hammersmith Bridge, which gave him the opportunity to look her directly in the face.

'You want me to pretend I love you, to be your boyfriend?'

'Pretend boyfriend. Just for a few months.'

'There's no one else to ask?'

'My mother intimidates my friends... in a friendly way,' she said with painful apology. 'No one would be able to withstand her interrogation without snapping and confessing to the truth.'

'Why not just tell her you're a grown woman—that you're not ready to get married and when you are, you'll choose your own husband?'

She looked dubiously at him. 'She's not wired to understand that. My entire life she has dreamt about my wedding day. I mean she's wonderful in all other ways, she just seems to think I need help in finding 'suitable' love.'

A honk alerted Ashley that the traffic was moving again. 'And what's in this for me? My life has to go on hold for two months while we pretend, that's no fun for me.'

'We'll still be able to see who we want, I'm not going to stop your love life... we just have to be careful people don't talk.'

'You haven't answered my question. What's in it for me?'

'Well, what do you want?' She looked at him sharply.

He didn't like having to bargain his way into her heart, but this seemed like his only opportunity to get past her frosty shields. 'Not much. Just to handle this with mutual respect, and get to know each other better.' His smile was slow and sweet, she fleetingly admitted, her eyes lingering on his lips.

Honey heaved a sigh. 'Give it a break, Ashley. I know all I ever want to know about you.'

'It's non-negotiable: respect and getting to know each other.'

'You drive a hard bargain,' she said tightly, but accepted, envisaging Sam Muller would be history soon and she would have no need of Ashley Elliott's service.

*

Party in the Park was held in conjunction with the local council, and Ashley's sound was booked for the entertainment. It was an unusually warm, end of September day and the crowds were out in force. Clad in colourful shorts, miniskirts, tight jeans and skimpy tops, girls of different sizes all competed for that celebrity look. In contrast, the Muslim women covered themselves in rich, flowing cloth, and the Asian women danced by in a flurry of startling coloured saris. Ashley, Dame and Richie had a large crowd going around the stage where their sound system was based, mostly screaming, dancing, laughing girls. Honey followed Fatty and Zhara onto the platform where the PA system stood to get a good view of the crowd.

'Look,' Fatty pointed, 'it's Sonny. He'd better keep out of my face, or I'll kick his shit! I told him this pregnancy is the last straw, so he better leave me alone.'

Honey suddenly felt awkward. Being on this platform meant she could see as well as be seen by the crowd. Everyone seemed to be watching Ashley. He was on the mic talking his DJ talk and the people loved it, dancing, gyrating and screaming to every tune he played, every word he said, every move he made. She couldn't help feeling a touch impressed.

'Now this one's for my girl, Miss Honey Elizabeth Fontaine,' he suddenly broke from playing Afro Beat to a slow jam. He threw her a look over his shoulder. Honey nearly died of embarrassment. She wanted the whole play as real as possible, but this was uncomfortable.

Ashley took off his headphones and handed them to Richie. He walked towards Honey, taking her hand and leading her behind one of the tall sound boxes. Then he pulled her in.

'We don't have to be this real,' she said, contradicting herself as she spotted Tracy Muller, Sam's big sister, and quickly wrapped her arms around him. Soon she got lost in the slow jam and her body moved against him with a mind of its own.

'This is what you do? This is your career?' she shouted above the music in his ear. He flinched.

'Sorry,' she said quieter.

'I'm a businessman, a promoter, an event planner and a producer. You'll need to know these things if we're to be in love.'

'I guess—'

'Come,' he released her and took her hand. 'Let's go get

a drink.'

'Back soon,' Honey shouted to Fatty.

Ashley put her in front, guiding her through the dense crowds with his hands on her shoulders. Their warmth made her tingle. He stopped at a stand to purchase two homemade pineapple smoothies and a litre of water.

'Honey!' Someone was calling her. Both she and Ashley looked around. 'Honey!' It was her Dad; she saw them now, her parents holding hands and pushing their way through the crowd towards her.

'It's my mum and dad,' she turned to Ashley.

'Shit! I'm not dressed right.'

She laughed, grabbing him back by the bottom of his shirt. 'You're too late, they've seen you. Let's check their reactions—just say hello and go.'

'We've been calling you from way back,' her father beamed.

'Didn't hear you.' Honey smiled. Then seeing her father's curious gaze at Ashley, she introduced him. 'Daddy, this is Ashley. Ashley, this is my father.' Her mother looked straight through Ashley as if he wasn't there. Ashley withdrew his hand from her and she felt his distance immediately.

Aaron Fontaine held out a friendly hand. 'Pleased to meet you. You must come around sometime, have a beer. Any friend of Honey's is welcome in our home.'

Ashley's smile relaxed as he shook hands. Fatty had told him Honey's step father was white and her mother stuck up. He didn't like the way Honey's mother was ignoring him—hating on him when she didn't even know him.

'Come on, Aaron.' Natasha tugged her husband's arm and began walking, 'Let's move on.'

Aaron flushed at his wife's rudeness. 'See you later, Honey... nice meeting you, Ashley.' His smile was apologetic.

Honey could tell Ashley felt insulted. 'I'm sorry,' she shouted above the crowd and music.

He didn't respond. He walked ahead and didn't look back to see how far behind she was. She struggled to keep up with him this time. When they got to a spot with some space, she grabbed his hand.

'I said I'm sorry. What's the big deal? So, we bumped into my parents and my overly friendly Dad invited you home. This is the whole point! You don't actually have to come! I'm not going to hold you to anything we do under this pretend coupling.'

He watched her without smiling, hands buried in the pockets of his jeans and head cocked to one side. She hadn't seen his face so serious before.

'I admit my mother is a snob—but she's not going to be in your life for long. Why has your energy changed? You think I'm going to fall in love with you?' she asked, smiling.

His heart surprised him. It lurched, jumped, danced. It did some crazy shit that was both frightening and wonderful.

'Your moms looks really young. Married herself a rich white man, huh.'

'Tasha was thirteen when I was born, and she married my dad when I was seven. I've never looked at him as a white man before, he's just Dad.'

Ashley held out a hand. 'Come, let's get back before Richie sends out the search party.'

As they walked towards the raised stage, Fatty came running by, her face coloured by rage.

'I'm going home,' she announced, marching past them.

'Hey, Fats, hold on.' Honey rushed after her and blocked her path. 'What's wrong?'

Fatty couldn't keep still. She turned to the left, to the right, she marched on the spot. She was livid. 'That bastard Sonny is telling people I have HIV. I feel so ashamed!'

'He's a waste of space. It's over between you two, just leave this one, Fats.'

Fatty wasn't convinced. 'I can't. He can't be going around chatting shit about me and thinking he can get away with it.'

'Just ignore him, everyone knows he's a fool.'

'I can't,' Fatty fumed. 'I just want to kick his arse.'

Honey linked her arm through Fatty's. 'We're getting too old for this. Let's go home.'

Honey looked back to see Ashley had resumed his place at the corner of the raised stage, headphones on his ears, playing music from his laptop. She hugged Fatty, trying to calm her as they forged through the crowd, but with one swift movement Fatty had lunged out of her reach and had pounced like a cat onto the back of an unsuspecting male. He was on the ground and people had scattered like a bomb alert while Fatty straddled him and used his head as a drumstick on the grass.

Honey stood rooted to the spot, horrified but not particularly surprised. She could see it was Sonny, and even though he was a good athletic build, he failed at untangling himself from Fatty's grasp. It took four burly security guys to eventually force Fatty off of a dazed, bloody and battered Sonny, who had to be assisted by paramedics. In the confusion, Fatty got free and ran, the crowd blocking the way of the security and allowing her to abscond.

Seven

September, 2015

Fatty lay on her single bed in her matching Bravissimo floral underwear, sipping directly from her ice-cold Guinness bottle, the contents she had mixed with rum and Red Bull. She needed it too after her melee with Sonny in the park. She had a hatred for men like Sonny: boastful, with a privileged entitlement to abuse women. When her phone rang it was the ringtone assigned to Honey. She was expecting the call.

'S'up?' Fatty said lazily.

'You okay?'

'Yeah. You? I see you and Ashley are getting it on.'

Honey laughed. 'Yeah, right. Tracey was at the Park, you know Sam's big sister, and I wanted her to tell him she saw me dancing and loved up. Tasha's introduction will be over before it's begun.'

Fatty struggled to sit up, fighting the tide of alcohol.

'I can't help thinking how lucky you are, Hon, having a mother that cares enough about who you marry. Tasha wants a rich, successful man for you. She's got a funny way of showing it but I think she really means well.'

'That's how I feel about Bella. I think your mother means well for you—'

'Hon. Stop. You have no idea, none whatsoever what you're saying about Bella. She ain't capable of thinking about nothing but her drugs, trust me on that. Anyway, you and Ash looked well-loved up, I almost believed you two were for real. I think tongues will be wagging, especially now he told the world about you over the mic.'

'As long as Tasha believes it, mission accomplished. So, I guess Sonny has some bruises by now. The police came after you left and he wouldn't give them any information, I think he's scared shit of you.'

'Good. Teach him to try and discredit my rep. I still don't feel I busted him up enough. There wasn't much blood.'

'Fat's, the man was bleeding. His lip was burst and both eyes were swollen. You fixed his arse, I'm telling you. And he wouldn't tell the feds anything.'

Fatty laughed for the first time since the incident. She had confirmation that she'd hurt him. Good.

By early afternoon Fatty was still apprehensive about leaving her house and going out. She had started to feel embarrassed about her fight with Sonny. When she eventually got dressed and entered her living room at minutes after 1pm, it was with the intention to cook a Sunday roast chicken with some sweet potatoes and broccoli, but her mother had a guest: a silver haired Asian man with a pot belly. Usually this would have been enough for Fatty to kick up a storm, insult her mother and leave behind a mist of the most toxic cussing any human being can articulate, but instead she decided to introduce herself and carry on with her plan to cook.

The Asian man responded to her introduction, 'I am Shankar.' His out held eager hand, devious hooded eyes and lop-sided smile spelt out to Fatty his absence of loyalty to the client who had no doubt been paid to give him a blow job. She knew this because that's all Bella gave, heads. Everyone knew that.

'I don't need to know you. Just get your money's worth from my sorry arse mother and get the fuck out of here... it's Sunday, a day of rest for most decent folks, and I want to cook my lunch, yeah! Are you married? Isn't your wife expecting you home for Sunday lunch?'

Shankar grew dark with discomfort and picked up his coat. 'You give me back money,' he told Bella, his right shoulder seeming to twitch involuntarily. 'I not stay here now, not after her,' he pointed accusatorily at Fatty.

'Go fuck yourself,' Bella spat. 'I'll still service you in my bedroom, you ain't getting no money back.'

'And you will perform this act knowing your child will be in this room?' Shankar seemed incredulous at this notion.

'Yes, she will,' Fatty chirped. 'She's been doing this since I was a kid. I know all about it so don't worry, the noise don't even bother me... she won't fuck you though, she only does blow jobs. And by the noises coming from her room, you'll leave your head in Mars.'

Shankar held his coat close, as though seeking comfort

from it. 'I will go. You,' he spoke to Bella, 'you keep money...' he turned to Fatty, 'sad life for child of whore.'

'Get the fuck out of my house.' Bella walked behind her stony faced punter, shouting and pushing him with her feet towards the door, 'You don't know nuffink about my daughter, you prick... and I bet you've got a little one too, I bet I wouldn't have been able to find your little teeny weeny prick. I bet you don't even have a prick. Get the fuck out!'

When Bella returned to the front room, Fatty was chuckling. 'You told his sorry piece of arse, but if you don't mind me asking, what the fuck are you doing for a man without a dick?'

They shared that joke, mother and daughter. Fatty was aware that there were sometimes the briefest of moments when she could forget her hatred for Bella and actually laugh at some of the things that took place in her home, but those moments were few and very far between. Mostly this, what she called home, was made up of a childhood of nightmares and patchwork dreams of escaping with her prince.

It was 3pm when she sat down to her Sunday roast chicken, sweet potatoes and broccoli. She ate alone because her mother had outgrown the ability to enjoy food. She only enjoyed coca cola, cigarettes, vodka, crack cocaine and heroin. Fatty thought she would have been dead by now but Bella just had the knack of surviving everything that could possibly go wrong, and she would bounce back again, like some broken jack-in-a-box character.

As soon as she finished eating, Fatty jumped into her second hand Mini Cooper, even though she hadn't technically passed her driving test yet. Whenever she got behind the wheel she would escape to heaven, her favourite Alicia Keyes filling the space and fuelling her dream. In no time, she was pulling into the cul-de-sac where Honey lived, half parking on the pavement because it seemed everyone had visitors. She fixed her hair in the mirror and ran her tongue over her teeth to remove any misplaced lipstick, for when she had to smile at Natasha. Fatty was intrigued by her. Natasha had been younger than Bella when she had Honey, disowned by her parents just like Bella, yet she didn't turn to drugs or alcohol or destructive relationships. Everyone knew Natasha turned to wealth when she married Aaron Fontaine.

Fatty looked up to the tapping on her window to see Honey.

'I was coming in to chill out with you,' Fatty said.

'Let's go. If we stay in, Tasha's going to make some excuse to come into my room and grill you for info on Ashley.'

'I don't know much, only that his dad ran off with some young thing and his Mum didn't take it too well. She's a recluse in a home somewhere, no one sees her.'

'Really? I don't suppose he has much time for the poor woman, and that family history would age Tasha twenty years. Don't say a word to her about him. If she ever asks, tell her you don't really know him and that I introduced him to you.'

Fatty smirked at the irony. 'Anyhow, let's go to Zeez.'

'That posh restaurant? Why?'

Honey looked smug. 'I just happen to know that Freddy Angelo, the manager, has a thing for you. It's my turn to do you a favour.'

'You're fucking with me,' Fatty kept her eyes on the road, 'but how does he know me? I don't know him. How do you know him?'

'He's the son of one of Tasha's friends. He's Brazilian and Italian mix—'

Fatty took her eyes off the road for a moment. 'Fuck! That is hot shit, Hon, hot shit. Brazilian and Italian—wow, that's like an Adonis... OMG... six foot with hot chocolate eyes, thick black wavy hair, six fucking packs for a stomach... tight bum cheeks... lips red like cherries... a dick the size of—'

'Fats, you are something else,' Honey laughed. 'Well, he's on Tasha's list of available young men for me but of course he and I have known each other since nursery and we just don't see each other in that way. Anyhow, Freddy says whenever he passes the record shop, if you're not busy serving customers and making them laugh, then you're giving advice and listening to people's problems. He wants to get to know you because he says by the way you day dream out of the window, you have bigger dreams than the record shop.'

'He saw that?' Fatty was incredulous.

Zeez was situated on the small but busy Portobello Road in Notting Hill and as Fatty turned onto the road and approached the restaurant, a red Corsa was pulling out of its parking space. She manoeuvred in quickly, ignoring the car ahead that was so obviously signalling and waiting to reverse into that space. The driver in the dark blue Alfa Romero honked his horn in angry successions but Fatty had already turned off the engine of her beloved car.

A tall, stocky, Black man got out of the car. 'Listen here, you can't steal a parking space from a person—' He was only on his second step before he stopped, his face contorting into a smile. 'Oh, it's you, Fatty. No problem, I'll find another parking space.' And he was gone.

Honey looked quizzically at Fatty.

'Don't even think about feeling sorry for that prick. He's a woman beater—only the last woman he beat was Za's cousin and they called me round to sort him out. And I did. I bust his arse!'

'Explains his reaction,' Honey laughed as she linked arms with Fatty, walking briskly towards Zeez. 'I so feel safe with you, Fats. You bust everyone's arse. Oh, look, that's Freddy's car driving in.' Honey was clearly excited and so was Fatty.

Eight

Ashley was agitated as he pulled up outside his accountant's house. He'd been avoiding Honey since the party in the park. He didn't take her calls or listen back to any messages she left. He wanted to walk away from her and the game she was playing on her mother, but was having great difficulties keeping her out of his mind. Fatty had tried to call him too. She'd even come to the studio. He had to have Dame tell her he was out of the country.

Marla's curtain moved and in seconds she was at the front door. A tall, curvy woman made attractive by the make up on her face. She had never been to college and hardly did school, but was a natural with figures and finance. Most importantly, she was trustworthy. He'd known her since he was fifteen years old, when he lost his virginity to her. She'd been eighteen and an excellent teacher, but all that was in the past. They had never revisited those times.

She adjusted her shoulder length blond hair, tugged at her mini skirt and opened the door wider as he approached.

'I need a drink.'

'Well, you're in one of those moods are you?' She closed the door behind him and followed him into her living room. 'What?'

Ashley flopped down on the soft, cream coloured sofa and closed his eyes. Honey's face was there. He bolted up. Marla held out a bottle of beer, and he drank half before placing it on the table.

'That bad, huh?' She eased him back on the sofa, sitting beside him.

Ashley could appreciate Marla's efforts to engage him, but Honey was all he could think of.

'I hear Richie has some beef with Tariq.'

'Richie has beef with everyone, ain't nothing new.'

She tried again. 'You see Fatty beat up Sonny? You know he goes round telling everyone that she has HIV.'

'Sonny says a lot of stuff and Fatty has history with him.' Ashley was not being hooked.

'Party in the Park went okay. I saw you there with your new squeeze, Fatty's friend. What's her name, the posh girl, lives in Ealing in one of them mansions, I hear?'

Ashley looked sideways at her. Did she know how he was battling his feelings for Honey? Did it show that he was having some internal conflict?

'She doesn't live in a mansion—it's just a house. Got any more beer?'

✳

Honey was pissed. Not being able to get hold of Ashley had made her irritable. She feared he might want to call the deal off, but did he have to ignore her calls because of it? Didn't he understand that this was only pretend? What was his problem?

Her mother's match-making attempts had escalated. She had been asking more about Ashley, but Honey had closed herself off, refusing to say too much, only that he would come to dinner soon.

'Well, until he finally decides to call you, we can lunch today,' Natasha said cheerfully. If things had waned between her and that boy, Natasha was all too happy about it. Her first glimpse of Ashley Elliot had done nothing to halt her anxiety about her daughter's new boyfriend or his agenda.

'Let's go Oxford Street shopping, my treat, then lunch,' Natasha suggested.

Honey usually loved to shop, but didn't feel like having to force excitement today and didn't understand why not hearing from Ashley had affected her this way.

'Can't face that crowd, Tasha. Can we do High Street Kensington?'

'Off course.'

'But I promised Fatty I would meet with her, so she'll come too.'

Natasha agreed good-naturedly.

Honey had to admit that shopping did have a feel-good atmosphere as she and Fatty walked arms linked ahead of Natasha, stopping to look at any and everything in the high street windows that caught their eyes. Natasha decided they should eat first and insisted on Zeez, the Italian restaurant in Kensington owned by her friend, Roberto Angelo, and his very beautiful, very Brazilian wife, Sabeena.

'You'll love the food,' Natasha told Fatty with a pat to her shoulder, 'and Fredrick is such a charmer. I think he and Honey would make a—'

'Tasha,' Honey interrupted, 'Fatty knows Zeez and she knows Freddy too.' Fatty and Honey exchanged knowing smiles as they took their seats in the restaurant at a table by the window. Fredrick brought them their menus. He wasn't the tall hunk Fatty had first imagined, the Adonis with six packs for a stomach. He was the same height as her in her three-inch heels, with a body that Fatty considered hunky but which many may consider chunky. His hair was shaved close to his head, with the tell-tale shadow outlining the bald patch in the middle, and he had his mother's beautiful features. Delicate jawline, straight nose and a thin top lip. He was good looking in her eyes.

'Hey Honey, nice seeing you.' He grinned at Fatty, 'Hi Vanesse.'

'Hi,' Fatty blushed.

'How's work, Honey?' Freddy smiled brightly.

'Good, only three months to go to end my probation. How are you coping with uni life in Manchester?'

'It's great. Returning as a mature student had its challenges, but I got used to it.'

Honey placed the menu card down and viewed him with interest. He was hanging back, trying hard to keep his eyes off

Fatty and keep his conversation natural in front of Natasha.

'Vanesse, you should try our lentil soup of the day. I guarantee you'll love it,' Fredrick addressed Fatty.

'Ok,' Fatty spoke in a small voice without looking at him. She was aware that Natasha was now viewing her with a disapproving scowl on her forehead.

It was clear that Fredrick had something on his mind, but it was obvious Natasha's presence was not going to allow it.

Honey took the matter in hand. 'Freddy, if you want to ask Fatty out, me and Tasha can give you five minutes alone.'

Fredrick smiled shyly and blushed furiously. 'Well, I was going to ask Vanesse if she'd like to have dinner with me here on Wednesday night, it's quieter.'

'Of course she would,' Honey butted in. 'Let's say 7pm?'

Fatty and Fredrick both nodded in agreement and Honey pulled him by the hand to sit down with them. As they continued with their friendly chat, heads close in some kind of conspiracy, Honey did not see Ashley walking past the restaurant. Ashley saw her though. It bothered him to see some guy talking in her ear. He walked away quickly before she could look out of the window and see him, before he could walk into the restaurant and make a big fool of himself.

'Join us for lunch, Freddy, you're the boss,' Honey encouraged.

Fredrick immediately stood up. 'Thanks, but I'm working and I have a new chef back there that needs my complete supervision.' He grinned, then smiled softly at Fatty. 'I'll call you later.'

Natasha watched him walk away disapprovingly. 'You and Fredrick have always got on. I thought—'

Honey made a face. 'Oh Tasha, don't even go there. We're friends, and it's plain to see who Freddy likes. Now let's eat and shop off this lunch.'

Back home, devoid of all the shopping bags, Honey and Fatty sat curled up together talking about Fredrick. Fatty would not believe that Fredrick liked her in that way. He was so far removed from her world.

'His family owns them posh Italian restaurants. To be honest, Hon, he's way out of my league. What should I talk about with him?'

'Just be your bloody self, that's who he likes. Don't try to be someone else or you'll lose him.'

'But I'm so fucking disgusting and ridiculous, he'll get sick of me soon if—'

'Oh, shut up Fats. There you go again, always putting yourself down. Freddy likes you! He told me he's liked you for ages. He's hot for you!'

Fatty felt flattered and dared to hope that perhaps she wasn't hard to love.

'I'm scared I'll make a fool out of myself, Hon. Come with me. Please.'

Honey viewed her with ridicule. 'No! He's harmless. Freddy is nowhere near as bad as Ashley Elliott, who you sold me out to. Go alone.'

'Then I won't go. I can't. He scares me.'

'Why?' Honey fumed.

'He's rich. He's clever. He'll see right through me. I couldn't stand that. I'd rather die or stay single forever than have someone so beautiful end up seeing me for what I really am.'

Honey sighed. 'You talk so much crap. Okay, I'll come for the first hour then you're on your own.'

'Okay. What should I wear? OMG, I have nothing to fucking wear.'

*

The following Wednesday they went along to Zeez and when Fredrick saw them, he was beside himself with joy. He settled them in the corner towards the back, which he assured were the best seats.

'This is where all the celebs want to sit,' he said proudly, pulling out a chair for Fatty, and then for Honey. 'May I recommend the house soup for starters? It's my father's recipe, and his mother and grandmother before that. It's delicious.'

'The lentil soup?' Fatty asked.

He smiled brightly. 'Yes. Did you enjoy it the last time?'

'Yeah, it was lovely.'

Fredrick was very shy around Fatty. Fatty had never been treated so much like a lady.

'So, you're back in Manchester in a week?' Fatty asked lightly, after a few drinks of liquid courage.

He nodded. 'Yes, but I'll be back once a month, and hope-fully you can both come and visit me some weekends.' He said *both,* but Honey knew he really meant Fatty.

'That sounds like fun,' Fatty smiled. She looked around the restaurant. 'This place is so posh,' she enthused, losing her previous fear. 'I would love to work in a place like this.'

'How would you like to take over my job? I'm looking for a manager. It'll be temporary, for a year until I finish my Masters, but by then I'm sure I'd need a deputy so you wouldn't be out of a job when I return.'

Fatty's eyes and mouth opened at the same time. 'Are you serious? You want me to manage this posh arse restaurant?'

Laughter brightened his face. 'Yes.'

'But I've never been a manager. I wouldn't know where to start. And I've never worked in a restaurant before.'

'You've got transferrable skills and you'll get training. You can start tomorrow if you like. I'll train you for the month before I go, and then we'll enrol you on some management training courses.'

Without thinking, she threw her arms around him and burst into tears. Fredrick liked the feel of her arms around his neck. She felt soft and smelt good.

'I'm so happy. No one has ever offered me such a dream job before. I promise you, I swear on my life, I won't let you down. How can I thank you?' She smiled through her tears.

Fredrick picked up a serviette and mopped at her eyes. 'By being the best manager this place has ever had.'

'I will,' she said in earnest. Then she threw her arms around Honey. 'I love you so much, my bestie.'

Nine

Honey was happy for Fatty and Freddy. In her mind they suited each other perfectly. Their adoration for each other was infectious, and made her think about what going serious with someone might feel like. Natasha was actively back trying to matchmake, having not seen or heard any more about Ashley Elliott. Honey had fooled Fatty and Zhara into thinking she hadn't cared about him not going through with their plan, but she couldn't fool herself.

Alone in her room, she tried to relax, flicking through magazines that failed to engage her, switching channels on the television, going on her laptop, checking out Facebook. She finally flopped on her bed, close to tears. *Why won't he take my calls? Why hasn't he called?* A tear slipped out, falling on the back of her mobile phone. It rang. She flipped it over and looked at the face. She rubbed her eyes in disbelief. It was Ashley! *Fuck!* It felt spooky. *What should I do? Pick it up? Talk to him as if everything's great? Cuss his arse out? Tell him to go fuck himself, who the fuck does he think he's calling over two weeks later? Selfish prick!* Her finger rejected the call. He rang again. She rejected it again. When it rang the third time, she turned the phone off. She wasn't clear what this would accomplish, and she certainly wasn't clear about what she would do if he never called again. All she knew for sure was that she never, ever wanted him to make her feel this way again.

Ashley was livid. He couldn't believe that the girl had cut off his calls and turned off her phone. It entered his mind to let her go, but then he remembered her smell, her lips, her hair, her way with words. The swell of her breast. He picked up his phone and called Fatty, who voiced exaggerated surprise.

'Ash! You're back in the country! Did you enjoy your trip? Where did you go? You brought us back a pressie?'

'Cut the shit, Fats. What's down with your friend?'

'Friend? Which friend? I have many friends. Who exactly are you talking about?' She smirked.

Ashley knew he would have to eat a little humble pie, after all it had been him who cut the communication. 'Hon-Hon. She ain't taking my calls.'

'I thought it was you who weren't taking her calls, not even my call. And when I came round to your studio you had your staffs telling me you're out the country when you were hiding in your fucking office.'

He was caught out. 'Okay, so I lied.' He sounded impatient. 'What's her game?'

'You better ask her.'

'How can I? She ain't taking my calls.'

'I can only pass on the message for you.' Her tone was

unsympathetic. 'You were the one trying to avoid her after agreeing to help her out. She's fucking pissed with you, although she's trying to pretend she's not.'

✳

Honey left work early Friday afternoon, making her way hurriedly to her car to avoid the grey October drizzle. She arrived at the car park to see Ashley leaned casually against her car, dressed all in chocolate and beige camouflage denim. Beside him was Dame, done up in straight red trousers tucked into flat leather Doctor Marten boots, and a Top Shop woman's jumper that stopped on his thighs. Her heart raced. She walked with a pretentious air of confidence, holding her head high and spearing Ashley with her eyes. *How dare he think he can just turn up like this.* Her heart danced.

'Hi Dame,' she smiled, always appreciative of his flamboyant nature.

'Hon.' He blew her a kiss. 'I'm not going to kiss your statuesque high cheek because Ash would have my beautiful bollocks transplanted elsewhere.'

She had wanted to stay sombre but that was near impossible when Dame was around. She laughed.

'Take your arse to the studio.' Ashley thrust his car keys at Dame.

'Ouch!' Dame feigned pain on catching the keys. 'You see how violent he is? My bollocks would be in problems in his hands.' He ran, taking tiny steps like he was on stiletto heels.

'You won't catch me,' he shouted back to Ashley.

As their icebreaker retreated farther away, silence reigned between them. Finally, Ashley spoke.

'Still mad with me?'

'What do you think?'

'Hanging up your phone on me, that's shit.'

'Yeah, you should know all about that.'

He looked around at the other workers coming and going. He couldn't believe the position he was in, practically begging for her attention.

'You finished for the day? Wanna go someplace with me?'

'Where?' She was super casual.

'Wherever you want. Let's just drive and sort out some of this shit.'

She drove around the narrow, winding roads of Twickenham until the tense silence became unbearable.

'Did you get freaked out meeting my mother? Tasha can be a snob, but it's a simple task I'm asking. Can you pretend to love me for a few months or not?'

He put one knee up against the dashboard and turned his head to look out the window, remaining silent. She had no idea what she was asking.

He sucked hard on his teeth. Honey was never far from his mind. He has never wanted to impress a girl as much as Honey Fontaine.

Honey rambled on. 'To be perfectly honest, I'd like it to be you because at least I feel I can have a level of trust in you, or I think I can... especially because Fatty does.' Her level of trust thrilled him.

He still couldn't shake the image of her with another man, but they were nearing his studio now and he'd have to make a decision—in or out.

When they pulled up outside the studio, she asked if she could come in.

'It's not really a place I'd bring a girl like you.' He opened the car door, then stopped. He took a strand of her hair and curled it around his finger.

'You're a diamond.' His voice softened. 'I'd take you somewhere fit for a queen.'

Relief filled her.

'Call you later,' he whispered, his voice hoarse with desire.

Ten

Shops and restaurants had already thrown up their flashing lights, Father Christmas figures, angels, elves and tinsels. Honey couldn't help but be filled with the festive spirit. She took the day off from work to go and support Fatty at her long awaited driving test. But before she drove to Kensington, she stopped outside A One Studio and rang Ashley. He came out, a half smoked spliff in his hand, and slipped into the passenger seat.

'What now?' He sounded cautious.

'It's time. You're coming for Christmas dinner and I'm not taking no. After this we can probably call it off.'

Her seeming indifference continued to unsettled him, but he was already in too deep. Perhaps Christmas would be his last chance to convince her this could be real. Honey carried on her day, oblivious to the storm of anxieties she had awoken in Ashley. It was a moist, cold day as she hurried into the warmth of Zeez, festively decorated with a silver and gold Christmas tree and a Mother Christmas, just as round and as jolly looking as her male counterpart. Fatty was sitting at the table looking nervous. She couldn't be still. Her fingers tapped uncontrollably on the table, her lunch of grilled jerk chicken and baked sweet potato sat neglected on her plate. There was not an empty seat in sight as it always was during the lunch period, especially the holiday ones.

'You've done great with this place, Fats. Your new Caribbean menu is popular.'

'I just want to make Freddy proud, Hon. He took a real chance on me and I don't think his parents really approve.'

'You will, don't fret so much. Christmas is near,' Honey slid into the chair facing Fatty. 'I've got an idea what to give Ashley for a present.' Her smile was a little wicked.

'Let me guess... er... pussy!' Fatty gave an exaggerated yawn.

'What's wrong with you?'

'I'm scared shit!' Fatty leaned forward to whisper. 'If I don't pass this time, I'll have to re-take the fucking theory again!'

'No-one wouldn't know you haven't passed your test yet, why do you always freak out when it comes to test time? All you have to remember is to use your mirror more and watch your speed.'

Fatty suddenly stood up and pushed her plate to one side. 'Let's go for a walk. I'm shaking like a leaf and I can't eat a thing.'

The winter sun was bright but the air cold and Honey pulled in closer to Fatty, shivering.

'It's times like this a few extra pounds come in handy,

eh,' Fatty teased, bouncing Honey with her hip. 'From inside you'd think it was boiling hot out here. I think I'm going to wear my sunglasses for my test.' She stopped suddenly. 'You think I'll be allowed to wear sunglasses?'

'I don't see why not.' Honey was still trying to tame Fatty's nervousness. 'You can't have the sun blinding you, that's dangerous.'

'But the tester guy may think me too bling and fail me. Oh fuck, look it's that bitch!'

Sonny's pregnant girlfriend, Stacey, was pushing a double buggy with two toddlers under three years old. The shopping bags on the handles meant she was walking slowly, as if she was going uphill. Her face looked carved out of exhaustion, which Honey didn't find surprising. Her grip tightened on Fatty as they grew level with Stacey, who had now seen them. Honey felt sorry for her. To be so young and have such huge responsibilities must be a nightmare. Stacey was only a year older than her, and about to have her third child—that really would drive sanity away.

'Hey, bitch,' Fatty chided, 'you look like shit!'

Honey tugged at Fatty to move her on, but her friend stood strong. 'Come on Fats, let's go.'

'No!' Fatty could still remember the embarrassment Sonny and this bitch had caused her over at Party in the Park, and the nerve of the girl to call her house to boast about her third bastard baby. 'If you ever phone my house again, I won't be responsible for what I do to you. Just thank your lucky stars you're breeding.'

Stacey may be a fool, Honey thought, but what she lacked in common sense had been compensated by her sharp tongue.

'Well, if you'd leave my man alone instead of putting your fat arse all over him, I wouldn't have to phone you, would I?'

Fatty pulled her arm away from Honey sharply. 'Your man! Sonny was mine before you were ever on the scene, stupid bitch!'

'Well how comes you didn't give him a baby? Because you can't breed! Sonny always said you're a waste.'

'Oh yeah! A waste, huh? Well why the hell does he keep calling my phone and sending me texts? Why ain't he living with you in your dirty little one bed council flat? I'll tell you why, because you're a dirty little slapper with no ambition!'

'Well, he keeps coming back to me too,' Stacey patted her small baby bump. 'And I've given him children!' She pointed to her toddlers.

'You and four others! And still he stalks me,' Fatty boasted loud enough to attract attention.

Honey was horrified at their public outburst. People walking past shook their heads in disgust, but most were very amused by it.

'Come on, Fats,' Honey pulled her arm, 'let's go before we end up on social media.'

Fatty shook Honey free. 'You,' she pointed at Stacey, 'need to get real. Sonny uses you for his blow jobs. And how do you think I know that? Because he tells me, stupid bitch! He beats your shit and I beat his! Who looks like the cunt now?'

'I'm going!' Honey retorted and marched away with big

strides. She loved Fatty, God knows she did, but sometimes, just sometimes, Fatty could be so infuriating.

Fatty hurried after her friend, laughing. She had never had such an opportunity to tell Stacey just what she thought about her.

'Hey, Hon, hold on. You get upset so quickly. I was really enjoying that.' Fatty, to Honey's dismay, was laughing, holding her side.

Honey came to an abrupt halt. 'I just don't understand what happened there.'

'I cuss it out!' Fatty retorted. 'And serves the bitch right! She's lucky she's pregnant or I'd kick the shit out of her!'

Honey shook her head in dismay. 'But why, Fats? You don't even want Sonny, you never have. Well, only for his money. But now you've got Freddy, so why behave like that?'

'Oh, come on, Hon, you sound just like Tasha! Loosen up.' She slipped her arm though Honey's as they began walking again. 'It's just a matter of pride, really. If you had a love and knew he bred some dirty whore who phones you with graphic updates, you'd have done the same.'

'No, I wouldn't, especially if I didn't really want him. And all that cussing in front of those poor children.'

'Well, I don't want Sonny but a cussing was long overdue for that bitch! Remember she used to phone my house leaving messages with Bella, dissing me all the time—I'm only giving her some of it back. You can bet her kids have heard far worse out of her and Sonny's mouth. Anyway, it's driving test time!'

*

Ashley called Honey later that evening. She was surprised.

'I thought you'd be stuck under some poor girl for the night. She got bored?' Honey chuckled wickedly.

'For someone who doesn't give a fuck about me you sure as hell are interested in my sex life.'

'I must admit, it does confuse me. Fatty says women line up for you, but you prefer solo?'

'I'll take that as a compliment. You want to eat with me tonight?'

'Why not, I was feeling a little bored.'

'You do know how to flatter a guy.'

It wasn't long before Ashley picked Honey up and took her to the new Caribbean restaurant that had opened in Mayfair: The Ackee Bowl Piano Restaurant, owned by one of his friends. The interior was warm and seductive, the lights soft but bright enough to see your food. Honey looked around appreciatively, loving the orange and chocolate colour of the walls and the beautiful 3-D waterfall mural. The chairs were leather backed and comfortable, the table cloth crisp and white against the brown straw table mats as mini candles flickered in their own little glass stands.

'Let's play lovers,' Ashley said, offering her a bite of a bread roll in his hand. Honey hesitated before indulging him. Soon he was feeding her and they were sharing food off each other's plate, their arms crossing as they fed each other.

'Ash! Glad you came.' Ashley looked up to see Corn-head,

dressed in his crisp white and blue chef uniform, grinning down at him and Honey. Ashley stood up and they greeted each other, touching fist then shoulder to shoulder before Ashley sat down again.

'Meet the better half of me.' Ashley lifted Honey's hand and placed it to his lips. She was surprised by an electric tingle that warmed her in a most private part of her body.

'I sense some sensuous tension going on here,' Corn-head laughed, revealing a single gold tooth at the top. 'It will need some sexual healing later.' He laughed louder, causing heads to turn towards their table. Corn-head turned to Honey, his face shining with wonder. 'Wow! You done it girl; you caught the big fish!'

'You have a lovely place,' Honey said, lost for words.

Corn-head's smile got even wider. 'Thanks to this man here.' He placed a slap on Ashley's back. 'Ash saw my potential and backed me financially. Wouldn't take a penny in interest.'

Honey couldn't help feeling impressed. Ashley was a conundrum, confusing and so contrary. He deliberately kept his eyes away from her.

'You gotta come play, Ash,' Corn-head told him, lifting him by an elbow, 'you can't tell me no.'

Ashley looked at the white piano that sat at the top of the restaurant like a VIP. Honey looked at him, puzzled.

'Ashley,' she said in an excited whisper, 'you play the piano?'

Ashley smiled at her. He liked it when he got her real attention, which he felt was rare.

'Sometimes,' he shrugged.

Corn-head was standing at the back of his chair, pulling it out. 'Come on, Ash, let's hear you play, it's been a while.'

Ashley relented and walked past the other diners to seat himself on the stool in front of the piano. He looked down at the keys and ran his fingers across them gently, like he was touching a woman's body... Honey's body. Everyone in the restaurant stopped eating to look expectantly at him. He closed his eyes and began singing.

Many rivers to cross and I can't seem to find my way over...

A round of applause filled the restaurant. Ashley looked up, embarrassed. He only ever played the piano alone or for his mother and sister. He didn't know what had taken hold of him. He got up and made his way back to Honey.

'That was beautiful, Ashley. I didn't even know you played the piano. A singing philanthropist? You are a dark horse.'

'Let's finish our food and go,' Ashley told her solemnly. His mood had changed but Honey couldn't understand his sombreness.

Eleven

December 2015

Christmas was Natasha's favourite season. It was the time of year when she hired an interior decorator to transform the house into something from Winter Wonderland. It used to excite Honey when she was much younger, but now it only exhausted her. Natasha wanted busy. She couldn't stand to see you sitting down, or even eating, when the decorations weren't complete. Once the decorating had been finished to Natasha's exhaustive standard, Honey and her father flopped down on the sofa with big sighs and a festive drink.

'So,' her father said, turning to her. 'Are we finally going to meet Ashley again? The only time we saw him was back in September, at Party in the Park. Is it serious between you guys?'

'Oh Daddy, you're impossible!' It was three months since her and Ashley had started *'dating'* and she was still dodging his official introduction to her parents. Honey had grown used to Ashley and, although she would never admit it to anyone living, her body could sometimes surprise her by responding to his cheeky ambiguities. She genuinely looked forward to seeing him too. He often took her to different clubs and restaurants, and let her pick the museums and theatres. It really did appear to people that they were a couple.

'Invite him for New Year's dinner too,' Aaron suggested.

'Maybe he has a family of his own to spend New Years with,' Natasha butted in, throwing her husband a look of annoyance which he totally ignored.

'Well, he can come for a couple of hours—grandma, granddad and the family would love to meet him, I'm sure,' Aaron insisted.

'Let him come Boxing Day,' Natasha rushed. She didn't want the rest of the family seeing the likes of him. She was hoping that Honey would have seen sense by now. 'I'd rather just close family members on Christmas day and News Years.'

'I've already invited him for Xmas.'

'Well tell him you made a mistake and we'll see him Boxing Day,' Natasha said firmly.

Honey agreed. She already knew Ashley wouldn't be coming Christmas Day. He was not looking forward to meeting her mother again and would most probably hibernate until spring after this.

Her phone rang and a quick glance told her it was Ashley. She walked out of the room to take the call. 'I was just going to call you,' she told him. 'Are we still on for the cinema?'

'Sure. I'll pick you up in an hour.'

*

Love Again

Only a red light lit the X room at the back of A One Studio. The usual crowd was there and so was a group of scantily dressed girls, followers of the DJs, girls from all over West London who had crushes on what they saw as successful men. The reggae music was loud, the room smoky from weed and saturated with the smell of alcohol and perfume. As the crew sat playing Fortnite, the scantily dressed girls sat on the other side of the room on the sofas. Bethany Collins was the only one modestly dressed in a cream leather trouser suit which showed no flesh, but which outlined her voluptuous shape. She was there for one reason only. Ashley. They had been a couple for over two years and she worshipped the ground he walked on. She remembered the weekends when she would coax him away from work, and he would cook for her. She missed his massages and his playful ways, and how she wanted another chance. His total love for work, for spending hours and hours in his studio and running his clubs, had left her lonely at times, and she admitted she was weak. She did what she had regretted ever since, had an affair with one of his business partners in south London. It crushed her that he never forgave her, that he wanted nothing to do with her and acted as though she didn't even exist. Like they hadn't spent good times together. She knew about Honey Fontaine. Everyone was talking about them. Bethany had seen Ashley with Honey in the club. She had also seen them at Party in the Park. Both times Ashley had ignored her, with his arm around Honey he walked past her as though she was invisible. Whenever she called him, he didn't take her calls. So, she did the only thing she could think to. She turned up at the X room. It took an age before she dared to approach him as he and his staff sat laughing about some YouTube video.

'Ash,' her voice was soft. She touched his shoulder and he turned around, frowning on seeing her.

'I'm going now,' she changed her mind. She was going to ask him to come home with her; she wanted to give him his Christmas present and maybe convince him to stay for a few hours so she could explain why she went to bed with Bruce Charles and how much she regretted it. But that look, the way he was looking at her, was so empty it made her shiver. She didn't want to mean nothing to him.

Ashley looked at his watch. He should have collected Honey ten minutes ago. 'I'm outta here, got things to do.' He stood up and slipped his arms in his jacket. Richie frowned. It was Friday evening.

'Where you going, Ash?' Richie asked. 'Friday nights we always hang together.'

'I'm on a move. Later.' Ashley didn't want to have to admit he was taking Honey to the cinema on their usual boys' night in. Richie would take the piss.

As he opened his car door, Bethany was by his side. 'Can you give me a lift home please?'

Ashley didn't look at her. 'I'm not going your way.' He opened his car door.

'Ash.'

'What's your problem, Beth?' He shut the car door hard, inserting the key into the ignition and starting the engine.

Bethany tapped on the window and he opened it. 'I want to explain about Bruce,' she pleaded.

'Beth. You slept with my business associate and he couldn't wait to tell me. I was hurt for a while. No, I was fucking hurting a lot for a long while. I'm over it now, you should be too.'

'What about that Honey girl? You've been seeing a lot of her.' Bethany let out the bitterness.

He drove off but not before his eyes sliced her in two. Bethany stood routed in a pool of pain, unable to stop the tears and wondering what she could do to make Ashley Elliott love her again.

*

Honey was impatiently pacing the icy pavement as Ashley pulled up to the curb. She opened the door and jumped in, rubbing her gloved hands together. 'You're late. It's really cold, must be near freezing.'

He turned up the heater. 'So, are we too late for the cinema?' He was hoping for a yes, so he could suggest his alternative.

She removed her gloves, pulled up the sleeves on her coat and looked at her watch. 'We could just make it.' She quickly pressed her lips into one of her funny smiles, melting him like ice on heat, and he drove to the cinema despite not wanting to.

He kept falling asleep. It was some boring love story but

Honey was hooked. Every now and again she used an elbow to prod him. 'Ashley, watch this part,' she whispered. He watched her at one point, totally engrossed in the screen, and his crotch hardened. What he wouldn't give to have her look at him like that.

As the screen went dark, even before the credits started rolling, Ashley sprang to his feet, grabbing Honey's hand and leading her out before the crowd could spring. What the hell he was doing in a cinema watching some soft romance movie would baffle him for a long time to come. They sat in the car while the engine warmed up and shared sips of Grey Goose and lemonade Ashley had ready in a glass bottle.

'That was really good, Ashley. You wouldn't know because you slept nearly all the way through it.'

'I don't do cinema—I'm old school. I buy DVDs from the Chinese girl and watch them in the comfort of my crib with my spliffs.'

'So,' she teased, 'I got you to do something you wouldn't normally. I'm honoured!'

He viewed her with interest, adjusting himself in the car seat; a new sensation whirled in his stomach. 'Now I want you to do something for me,' he said, pulling the car slowly out of the car park. 'Ready?' He held his head straight.

'What is it?' she asked, watching his profile as he drove, wondering what it would be like to make love with him and she knew the alcohol was loosening her. 'You're coming home with me... now... spending the whole night.' He halted at the traffic lights and turned to watch her for fear, or protest. Her lips parted into a slow smile.

'Is that why you let me drink most of the Grey Goose? Because you want to bone me?'

Ashley shook his head in disbelief. 'I didn't drink so much because I'm driving, and I didn't force you to drink.'

She wasn't surprised by his ground floor flat situated behind iron gates in South Kensington. It was modern, minimalist and practical. It was a well looked after home. Men, she knew, were not normally this tidy. In fact, some of them were plain nasty.

'All this time and I never knew you lived here?' She crossed her arms looking at him.

'I don't bring anyone here.' He took a step to face her, unfolding her arms, his fingers unbuttoning her coat. She allowed him to remove it, placing it carefully over the arm of the sofa. 'It used to be my brother's flat; I bought it from him at a family price.' He chuckled.

She walked unsteadily around the spacious and well decorated living room, while he disappeared into the kitchen. 'You have style,' she commented, running her hand along the magnolia walls which lent warmth to the room, matching the leather sofa. It smelt like him, the room. Like his clothes. That fresh, sharp woody scent of his cologne and the smoky smell of marijuana. Under her feet was white, shiny marble tiled floor, partially covered by a grey and black rug. Then a black shiny piano took centre stage, proclaiming its importance. Other than the huge wide screen television fixed to the wall, there was only what she presumed to be a family picture.

His mother, a very thin, very sad, blond-haired woman; his younger sister, a shy pre-teen; and Ashley in the middle, his arms around their shoulders, looking very protective of both.

His arms circled her from behind. 'A drink to warm you.' He placed a glass of wine in her hand.

'Is that your mother and sister?' She was staring at the picture.

'Yes.'

'Where do they live?'

He moved to sit at the piano. 'My sister lives with my aunt in Acton but my mother is in Barnes, near Hammersmith.' His fingers were playing odd notes. He couldn't sit at a piano and not play it.

'I loved when you played *Many Rivers to Cross*,' she told him, moving in close. And so, his fingers began the journey across the white and black keys like a fluttering butterfly. She sat and listened, watching as the music he was making took him out of the room to somewhere she couldn't see.

'It takes you somewhere when you play that,' she whispered.

'It takes me to my mother's smile,' he said, then got up abruptly and walked over to the CD player, pressing buttons so the green light winked and music poured into the room. He took her hand and began a slow sensuous dance against her.

'Take off your clothes. Let me see all of you.'

'I'm not that drunk,' her head rolled off his shoulder and he caught her before she could fall. 'You know I think I've overdone the alcohol,' she told him slowly so that the words sounded how she wanted them to. 'I'm going to trust you not to do anything I might regret and hate you forever for. And I mean forever.'

Ashley smiled and scooped her in close, placing small kisses on her cheeks, lips and neck. He'd not been this intimate with her before. He'd danced with her, known the feel of her waist, the feel of her breasts pressed against him, her arms around his neck. But it had all been in a dance. He let his hand run over her bottom, pulling her in and engulfing her lips with his. She kissed him back, slow and sure in what she was exploring. She wound her hands around his neck and took in his lips, allowed him to take hers, and didn't stop him as his hand slid under her tee shirt and cupped her breast. The dizzy haze of desire was chaotic.

'I'm going to trust you not to do anything I'll hate you forever for,' she repeated in his ear as Ashley lifted her into his arms and carried her into the bedroom, spinning her around and around. When he gently laid her down her eyes were closed. She was sleeping, a soft, low snore coming from the back of her throat. It was mid-morning when she opened her eyes. She felt Ashley behind her, spooning her, and she glanced down at his hand loosely around her waist. She was fully dressed. Honey smiled, relieved to find her clothing was still on her body and there was no tell-tale feel of the aftermath of sex.

She turned around into his arms and his amber orbs met her with the warmest welcome a pair of eyes had ever emitted. She untangled herself before she could fall into him.

'We're getting to know each other as you wanted. I'm glad I trusted you. Thank you, Ashley.' She wasn't sure what she was thanking him for—surely not for the simple act of not having sex with her while drunk. No, it was the intimacy of softly waking up in his arms. Her eyes held onto his and she was more confused than ever now. He found himself feeling deeply content in her gaze. Honey Elizabeth Fontaine was going to be a force to reckon with.

*

Boxing Day found Ashley sitting casually in the Fountaine's lavishly furnished Ealing home. He sat, feeling uneasy, on the marigold soft leather sofa, despite his relaxed manner. The thick Arabian mat under his shoeless feet was made of differing shades of the earth, varying between terracotta and gold, covering the real wooden floors, which were of course smoothly sanded and varnished, adding to the smell of the house. He was told to remove his shoes by Honey on entering the living room and he did. He viewed the paintings on the wall. They were all pink and white skinned cherubims, angels, landscape art, or art that would take a few drinks to decipher. His first impression of Natasha was that she was some wanna-be, marrying a white man and giving her Black child a white Daddy. Nothing he saw now changed his mind. He smiled when his eyes rested on an inevitable family portrait. Honey must have been about eleven years old, sat in the middle of her smiling parents. Next to it was a more recent one of her graduation, flanked by her parents.

The daggers coming from Natasha's eyes were clearly visible. Ashley was once more surprised at how young she looked—more like an older sister than a mother.

It broke Natasha's heart that the man her daughter chose to fall in love with had dreadlocks. It didn't matter that he was so incredibly good looking, owned his own business and drove a car she approved off. His locks rendered him some kind of drug don in her eyes. Some undercover, gun-trotting thug, who Operation Trident should know about.

The atmosphere was strained, Natasha's naked disapproval was unnerving for Ashley and by the end of his first drink, he was ready to go but held out for the sake of Honey and the effort being made by her father.

'You know in my twenties I was in a reggae band, bass player, could have given UB40 in the 80s a run for it,' Aaron boasted, breaking the silence that had once again fallen.

'I can see that,' Ashley said, sitting forward on the sofa, clasping his hands. Natasha had been eyeing his relaxed posture in her chair with a frown which he tried to ignore. 'Bass player, huh, do you still play?' Ashley showed more interest than he felt.

'Not in a long while. I think I may still have some recordings,' Aaron was quite excited at having someone to talk to who seemed impressed by his past musical efforts. 'I'll look them up and the next time you come, I'll let you hear them. They're all on a DAT machine though. Afraid I'm a bit behind times.'

'I could copy them over to CD if you like,' Ashley offered.

Aaron beamed. He relished the thought of hearing his old band again. 'That would be great.'

Natasha stiffly told everyone dinner was ready. She had sliced the turkey from Christmas day leftovers, roasted some potatoes, baked half of a salmon and a macaroni cheese, roasted carrots and parsnips and steamed down some broccoli. Honey held Ashley's hand as he took his place around the large dinner table. Why they needed such a big table with twelve chairs when there were only three of them, he would never ask. Honey spooned a small portion of roast potatoes, a slice of salmon, the vegetables and salad onto Ashley's plate. She poured him a large glass of white wine and sat close to him. She could see he was near to being pissed off.

They ate mainly in silence, Aaron trying a few times to make conversation with his wife, to include her in the talk he was striving to keep up with his daughter's boyfriend. Ashley toyed with the food on his plate. He wasn't hungry, but didn't want to offend Honey. Then Natasha did what Natasha was good at doing, speaking her mind.

'So, Ashley, do you smoke weed? Have you ever been in trouble with the police? How did you get the money to own a club and a studio? Drugs, maybe?'

'Natasha!' Aaron exclaimed, shaking his head at his wife.

'Tasha!' Honey barked. 'Please!'

Natasha didn't care. He wasn't the man she wanted for her daughter. He had the wrong image: dread-locked and weed-smoking, no doubt. Honey had no idea, her mother felt sure, of what such a boy could do to her self-esteem, her heart, her very soul. Natasha assessed that her most vulnerable time was her first time in love, her first taste of kisses and sex— her first man, Kishan McNeely, Honey's father, who too had dreadlocks.

'It's okay, I'll answer Natatrash's question,' Ashley said curtly. He hid the smile that threatened to tug his lips at the annoyance on her face at his mispronunciation of her name. 'It may surprise you but I've never been in trouble with the police. I'm DBS checked because I also work with the council in schools with kids. And my business is a legitimate promotion and entertainment company, which started off with local government funding before I became self-sufficient.' His eyes held Honey's for an age.

'Really?' Natasha took him on, opening her eyes in mock surprise. Her tone was suggestive, heavy with sarcasm. Why didn't he just go? Hadn't she shown enough discourtesy to drown a whale? She knew she couldn't choose her daughter's love, but she wasn't going to encourage this one. A dread-locks man with a hobby—playing music for a business could not be taken seriously.

'I was quite surprised to see how... young you look,' Ashley spoke with spikes in his voice. 'Here's Hon twenty-eight and there's you looking thirty.'

Honey sucked in her breath, her heart sinking to her feet. She looked at her clasped hands on her lap, any hope of an amicable relationship between her pretend lover and her mother now lost.

Natasha knew which angle he was coming from. Pillow talk, no doubt. When a naive girl, such as her daughter, was in the devious arms of a charmer like him, she spills her family history like a young virgin pouring oil into a cobra—who will eventually hiss it out with venom in her face. He obviously knew there wasn't a great age gap between her and Honey.

'I had Honey at a young age.' She challenged him with her steely eyes. 'I was young, vulnerable and stupid. I believed a liar who left me pregnant and helpless. Lots of them around, liars,' she said meaningfully. 'But looking back he had an excuse. He was also a teenager, so teenage behaviour is to be expected.'

'It doesn't have to be the same for everyone,' Ashley spoke quietly, thinking that it was time he made his exit. Honey's mother had issues.

'Are you saying you're serious about my daughter?' She was spooning broccoli onto her plate. If only she could let Honey see him as she could.

'Hon and I are doing fine, one day at a time.' Ashley smiled weakly at Honey, feeling sorry for the predicament she was in. He regretted already rising to Natasha's bait, and didn't want to make things any worse.

'You hear that, Honey? Did you hear his answer? What he's really saying is he has no intention of taking you seriously. You can do a whole lot better than...!' She threw a hand towards Ashley.

Ashley stood up abruptly. That was it, he needed to go before he said anything he might regret.

'Natasha, that's enough!' Aaron said sternly. 'Don't go treating Honey's guest like this.'

Natasha smirked, enjoying the fact that she had rattled him.

'Thanks,' Ashley turned to Aaron, then stood up and left the table. Honey ran behind him, throwing her mother a cold look.

'Ashley, don't go. Don't leave like this, or she wins,' she pleaded.

He put on his shoes and headed out the door.

'Ashley, please! Don't be like this with me.'

He stopped and turned to look at her. She had run after him barefoot on the cold ground.

'Go inside, you'll catch a cold. I'll call you later.'

She could see he was tense with anger; she was angry with her mother too.

'Is our deal off? Are you angry?'

He involuntarily softened as her anxious eyes scanned his face.

'No.' He touched her hair, entwining a strand around his finger. 'You never make me angry... just crazy.' He smiled. 'Go on inside, your feet,' he pointed.

Honey walked back inside, realising how cold her feet had become. She couldn't eliminate the feeling of rejection again. Despite the closeness they seemed to share, Ashley was like the shifting desert sand. One moment he would look at her and she would see such tenderness in his eyes that she felt fear. Yet there were times when she wondered if he liked her at all; he could be so cool that uncertainty would go for a cross country run through her heart.

'Tasha, how could you be such a bitch?' Honey burst back into the dining room where her parents were still sitting. She walked to stand in front of Natasha, arms on hips and a foot tapping.

Natasha knew when her daughter looked at her in that way, a storm was brewing. 'Sit down, Honey, and watch your language. Don't talk to me like that,' she said, sipping her white wine.

'I'm going to watch a bit of TV,' Aaron excused himself.

'Why couldn't you even try? Why?' Honey was angry. 'You made no effort at all.'

'I know,' Natasha admitted calmly. 'I'm sorry it hurt you, but I'm not sorry it happened.'

'But why? You don't even know him and you decided not to like him.'

'I know his kind,' Natasha said flatly.

'And what type is that? Like my father, my real father?'

'One day you might thank me,' Natasha told her.

'For what? Ruining my life? I'm a grown woman and I can choose my own love. Just stop trying to arrange my life and marry me off to your friends' sons, it's humiliating. I can choose for myself!'

Natasha stood up and picked at some imaginary fluff on her jeans. 'He's not right for you, Honey—'

'How do you know? You clairvoyant or something?'

'I've lived a little longer than you.'

'Not much,' Honey snapped.

Natasha sighed. 'We'll have to agree to disagree about him, but I know I'm not wrong. He's wild, Honey; he's got dreadlocks and he's in the entertainment business; he won't thank you for caging him.'

'So, you're prejudiced because he's a promoter and not a banker? Because he's got dreadlocks and not cut to the scalp hair? It's the twenty-first century, Tasha, and you got to embrace the changes and stop conforming to stereotypes! And for your information, I don't want to cage him. I just want to love him.' Honey's heart leapt at the truth that had escaped. Natasha despaired at her child's gullibility.

Twelve

Ashley had to plead with his little sister to come out of his car as they sat parked in front of the house where their mother now lived in Barns, South West London. Marley was sullen and close to tears, arms tightly crossed as if holding in her insides. She stared unseeing out of the windscreen, her caramel skin glowed with youth, her rounded cheeks made more prominent by the fact her hair was swept up in an amateur bun on the top of her head.

'She doesn't even like me and I hate it here,' she protested. 'It's full of loonies.'

Ashley turned her face sharply to him using one finger on her cheek.

'Ouch, that hurts.' She slapped his hand away.

'I'll hurt you more if you ever use that word again. Your mother isn't a loony and she doesn't hate you.'

'Then why she got to live here and take all them medication? She's a nutter! And she does hate me; she only loves you and Nate and the husband that left her arse.'

Ashley opened the car door abruptly and got out. He walked around to the passenger side and yanked the door, taking Marley by the arm and firmly pulling her out of the car.

'If I hear you speak like that about your mother again, I'll wash your fucking mouth out with pepper!'

'Get off me Ash, I'm gonna tell Auntie Dawn.'

'And when I tell her what you called your mother, she'll beat your black arse blue!'

'Actually, it's a mixed-race arse,' Marley said, smartly.

Holding her firmly by the wrist, he marched up to the big green oak door and held a finger a little too long and too hard on the bell. The door opened slowly and a young, pale woman in her early twenties, bloated by medication, with hair uncombed toppling onto her shoulders, eyes dark and troubled, looked quizzically at them. Her face suddenly released its anguish, her cheeks giving way to dimples as a smile of recognition took its place.

'Ash, Ash, your mam's here, she's been making lots of trouble,' the young woman stepped to one side, beckoning frantically for them to come in.

Ashley pulled Marley inside with him. 'Hey Suzie, you doing okay?'

Suzie became self-conscious, raising a hand to smooth down her greasy hair and undoing a button on her stained and creased blouse. 'I'm okay. Your mam's not come out of her room yet and she won't take her meds. Pete and Mrs Reece have been trying to get her to.'

Alton Hall was a large, characterless house that could

easily be used in a horror movie, with the right touches added. Despite its clean, pristine walls and the shampooed carpet, the rose scented disinfection couldn't quite conceal the distinct odour of urine and unwashed bodies. The furniture was sparse in the large communal lounge. A book shelf, two three-seater sofas that faced each other, a coffee table and bare magnolia walls. When his mother had been placed here by social services, he'd asked why there were no pictures or paintings, only to be told that the inhabitants' state of mind meant pictures deemed beautiful to normal minds could represent quite scary things for them.

'Ash, Marley, hi.' Mrs Reece, the manager of the house, held out a small, plump, pink hand, smiling broadly and revealing smoke stained teeth. Ashley shook her hand. 'Suzie tells me mom's playing up again,' he smiled.

'Afraid so. Hasn't taken her meds in two days, but I know you'll be able to change that. She's up in her room and refuses to come out. She's eaten very little in the last two days.'

'Say no more.' Ashley, still holding onto Marley, started walking towards the stairs.

The winding stairs took them up to the first floor where his mother's room was situated. He knocked lightly on the door before opening it, still holding Marley's stiff and protesting hand. The smell of frankincense and myrrh filled his nose; his mother always got the staff to burn it, to stave off demons. His face fell. His heart broke. At least the curtains were open; it gave hope because if her room was in total darkness, that's where her mind would be. She was lying still on the bed, her

97

short grey hair messy, her hands crossed on her abdomen, looking thin and wistful.

'Moms, what's going down?' Ashley pushed a pillow to one side and sat down beside her on the bed.

Her blue eyes were dull and confused. 'Ash. You've come to see me. You look so like your dad,' her face softened.

'Why are you lying down? Let me help you to sit up.' He puffed up two pillows and assisted her to sit against them. Ashley pulled Marley towards them.

'Marley's here, Moms. Come and kiss your moms, kid.'

Marley stiffly and dutifully placed a dry kiss on her mother's unresponsive, alabaster cheek, before hastily stepping back out of her sight.

Ashley moved towards his mother, reaching both hands out to smooth her grey, unkempt hair, which in his childhood was a lustrous brown. She leaned forward and rested her head against his chest.

'Moms, you know you gotta take your meds.' He cradled her, rocking her gently as she clung to him.

'I didn't mean to chase your dad away. There's a dark demon in my head. I need him to go. He says I've got to come home.'

Ashley kissed her forehead. 'You didn't chase that man away, he left us. Now if you take your meds, the demon will go, I promise, and you'll be able to come home.'

She moved out of his arms, her face crumbling. 'If only your dad would come home and forgive me. I would be good again, like when we first married.'

Ashley stood up swiftly and took her by the hands, looking down into her tear-blurred, blue eyes. He stroked her cheek, the soft feel taking him back to his childhood. 'You've done nothing wrong; he's the one who should be begging your forgiveness. Don't I take care of you, Moms?'

'Yes, but you're a child, Elliott is—'

He dropped her hands. 'Gone!' he spat. 'He's gone, Moms, and I'm a grown man.'

Her lips quivered and the tears rolled. 'Gone? He left? I chased him away.'

Ashley thrust his hands into the pockets of his jeans and turned his back. Marley looked very bored and untouched by her mother's anguish.

'You know he left, Moms, even before Marley was born, he left us. I've been looking after us and I'm still looking after us. You didn't chase him, he left us!' He spun around, his teeth sinking into his bottom lip, his eyes pleading and moist.

She nodded. 'You're a good boy, Ash, a good boy. The demons are coming, you know. You must find love, so it doesn't get you too. You have a girlfriend?'

'No demons will get me. Let's get the meds to keep them from you, come.' He held out his hand to her.

She looked down at his hand and hesitantly placed her own in his. 'You must get a girlfriend and love her, so the demons don't come. They say some really crazy things.'

'I'll stop them, I promise, but you've got to take your meds so you can come home.'

She smiled up at him and allowed him to lead her out

of her room, Marley following behind. Downstairs in the communal dining room, Mrs Reece brought the medication in a small white cup in one hand and a glass of water in the other.

'Glad to see you up and about, Doreen.' She smiled, placing the tablets in Doreen's outstretched hand.

'My son is here. Ash has come to see me. He chased the demons away and he's got a girlfriend, she'll keep the devil away.' She put all the pills under her tongue and drank down the glass of water, squeezing her eyes shut until they bulged. Slowly she opened her eyes and smiled.

'You have a very good son,' Mrs Reece beamed. 'Would you like to help Trevor with the cooking today?'

Doreen swirled around like a ballet dancer would. 'As long as it's curry chicken, I want curry chicken.'

Ashley held his mother's hand and walked her towards the large French windows and outside onto the huge lawn. The winter sun was strong and the grounds were alive with splashes of colourful bluebells, and cherry blossom trees. The green hedges were tall and bushy, but well maintained, and benches and tables congregated in one corner. His arms circled his mother's shoulders as they walked, and he beckoned to Marley to fill his other arm.

'Is it winter or spring?' Doreen viewed the blue bells in confusion.

'It's winter—but they say global warming means the seasons get confused,' Ashley offered.

'You have a girlfriend? Oh, Ash that would be good. You

never bring a girl to see me. Are you ashamed of me?' asked Doreen.

He cleared his throat. 'No. Actually, I want you both to meet someone. Her name's Honey and we get on well.'

'Don't hurt her, Ash, don't hurt her.'

Ashley squeezed his mother's shoulder and kissed her cheek. 'She's too smart for that. She's funny and beautiful, clever and mouthy... you'll love her.'

On the drive home from Barnes, Marley's arms were still tightly crossed. She looked lost and confused and tearful, as she did after most visits to see her mother. Ashley was used to it. Crossing over Hammersmith Bridge, they encountered traffic, bringing them to a crawl.

Ashley pushed the button to wind up the windows, wrinkling his nose. He turned his head to his sister.

'You okay, Baby Sis?'

Marley shook her head and pulled a tissue out of her pocket, wiping her eyes. 'I'm never okay after seeing her. She doesn't even like me; why do you make me?'

Ashley drove steadily, nodding his head and biting his lip. 'Because she's our moms; she's all we got and we're all she's got.'

'But she doesn't want me, Ash. She just ignores me, like I'm not even there... and why do you always make me have to kiss her? I just know she doesn't want me kissing her either, she cringes.'

Ashley breathed out heavily, shaking his head. 'That's not true. Moms's sick, Marley. She's messed up in the head, she doesn't think like you and me... she thinks in her own pictures.'

Marley shifted her body to face his profile as he came to a red traffic light. Ashley pulled up the hand brake and smiled weakly, shrugging his shoulders.

'She blames me for Dad leaving, she hates me for it.'

'Yes, she does, but that's because she can't face the truth. You can't keep a man who don't want you. Our father didn't want our moms.' Ashley saw a break in the traffic and swerved into the lane. 'He didn't want her and he didn't want us!' Ashley's grip on the car wheel tightened. 'Our moms' sick, Baby Sis. Her reality is blurred and her heart is broken. That's why she's the way she is.'

The traffic began to gather speed as Ashley got over the bridge. He lowered the window and crisp winter air filled the car.

'I won't let no guy break my heart and turn me into a loony. If he leaves me, he can go to hell for all I care. Your mom's weak.'

Ashley sighed. 'Yes, she is,' he nodded in agreement. 'That's why she needs us.'

'She needs you, not me and I don't want to talk about it. Can I ask you something? Is your girlfriend Honey special? More than that Bethany?' Marley sniggered.

'Two very different women, Sis.'

'I'm glad you've got someone; you were so grumpy after you and Beth split. With your looks you should have lots of girls—all the year 11 girls at my school say so.'

Ashley took his eyes off the road for an instant to view her.

'What did you say?'

'Ash, the girls in my school talk about you all the time, especially the girls in Year 11; they all want a piece of you. You're supposed to be this handsome millionaire.'

'What! What are you kids learning in school these days? You'd better stay away from those kinds of girls and don't make me have to come and talk to the Head Master.'

Marley's smile was genuine for the first time that day. 'Of course, Big Bro. You're the man.'

'And I'll just let you into a little secret: Honey isn't my girlfriend. We're pretending so her Mom stops trying to marry her off.'

'Is she Muslim?'

'No, I guess that's Hon's point. Her mom's Black Brit but snobby. Her real father is Ethiopian. Her mom's married herself a rich white man and wants to marry her daughter to money—that's the way it looks to me.'

'I wish I had a mom who would be that interested in me.'

Ashley smiled cheekily. 'At least you have me. I'll be showing a lot of interest in any boy you like in the future.'

Thirteen

March 2016

Nearly seven months on, Natasha still had nothing civil to say to or about Ashley. She was sick with worry that he and Honey were still together in what she considered to be a peculiar relationship. There was something about their relationship that felt casual and odd. She couldn't understand why Honey couldn't, or wouldn't, see it.

'Honey, are you going out again tonight? That's three nights in a row and you have work tomorrow.'

Honey's hand was already opening the door. 'Tasha, give me a break... I'm all grown, I don't need you to watch over me. I'll see you later.'

'What time?'

'Tasha! Please, just stop doing this. I can look after myself.' She kept her back to her mother.

Natasha folded her arms, shaking her head and letting out heavy sighs. 'You can't even wake yourself up for work! If me or your father don't wake you up, you sleep right through your alarm.'

Honey opened the door wider, glancing sideways at her mother. 'See you later, Tasha.'

'Can I tell Rachel that you'll come to her 50th birthday party?' Natasha asked quickly, following Honey to the door.

'Why? Because you want to matchmake me with her son Liam? I'm dating someone, as if you don't know.'

Natasha waved a hand dismissively. 'You can't be serious about that boy—'

'Suppose I am,' Honey cut in. The whole pretend thing had continued because Natasha hadn't given up trying to arrange a suitable boy for her, and because Honey had started feeling comfortable playing Ashley's girlfriend, which she would of course deny if ever confronted.

'You deserve better. There's just something very not straight about him—'

Honey opened the door. 'Not sure how you came to that conclusion... but just maybe I'm the one using him.'

Honey sat sulkily in the passenger seat of Ashley's newly acquired, Porsche sports car. Traffic was sporadic and as he drove, Ashley kept taking his eyes off the road to glance at Honey.

'S'up, Hon-Hon? You're kind of quiet...' He nudged her playfully.

Honey huffed, pulling a face at him. She fell silent and turned her head to look out of the window, taking in nothing.

'Your crazy-arse manager pissing you off again? Just say the word and we'll set Richie on the smurf. That's what you guys call her, right?'

'Didn't we agree that you'd keep any woman on the low? Why is Tasha's friend telling her she saw you in some estate agency with a woman whose dress could be called a blouse, it was that short?'

He laughed good humouredly and gently flicked her ear. 'You women make me laugh. Your mother's friend obviously has nothing better to do than mind other people's business. That was Marla, my accountant. I'm looking to buy another property and that's her thing, she's advising me. Are you jealous?'

'Hell no! I just don't want to look like a fool.'

'I would never do that, even if it's just pretend.'

He sounded so serious she looked at him for a few more seconds than she wanted to.

'You said a few months. It's been over six months and we're still pretending... you could have been more than half way to giving birth to my baby by now.'

Honey looked humoured. 'That would be a disaster. You don't strike me as the fatherly type.'

'Why not just tell your mother you'll choose your own man?'

'I've told her, hundreds of times, but it makes no difference.' She sighed. 'You may be right. We should just call this whole charade off.' She really didn't mean it, her heart beat anxiously as she waited to see if he would object, to confirm if what she sometimes felt from him was real. 'I think if it was any other guy I was pretending with, Tasha would've given up by now... but there's something about you that makes her relentless in trying to get me away from you.'

Ashley knew this only too well. 'Do you think she would approve of me if I were completely white?'

'What a thing to say. No, my mother isn't like that. She tries to fix me up with her Black friends' sons too.'

The traffic started moving. Ashley put the car in gear and rolled along slowly. 'Well, maybe we should move it up a level, spend more time together.'

Honey sniggered, placing a strand of hair behind her ear. 'You're kidding me, right? See you more often? We get on each other's nerves, we—'

'I know, and I don't know any way around that, but if you're desperate to get back to your life, let's give it a last go.'

Honey sighed dramatically. 'I think we should get back to our lives. I don't want to put you through torture by spending more time with me.'

Ashley concealed his need to smile. 'Truth is I like spending time with you, as mouthy as you are. We piss each other off equally, so I guess we're a match.'

He turned off the A40 and back into a lighter traffic flow. He took the back roads into Hammersmith, passing tree lined roads, and for a duration they were quiet.

'So, what does spending more time together look like?' Honey queried, concealing her mounting excitement.

'Going out more. You can come down the club more often so people will see us together, we can go eat out more, you can introduce me to some of the things you like, even go for a weekend away some place, no one would have to know.'

'Okay. But who's paying for these increased dates and weekends away?'

'I'll pay—treat you the way I'd treat my woman.'

Honey looked taken aback. 'Really?' Her gaze was steady, searching.

His eyes twinkled with mischief. 'Yes—how I feel about you—you make me want to try different things. Like now, you know what I want to do?'

'What?' She heaved, viewing him suspiciously while leaning away from him.

'Follow that number 33 bus, see where its crazy-arse takes us. We follow it to the end of its route, then we turn around and drive back to my place, where if you're really, really entertaining on this drive, I'll let you strip me butt naked and have your wicked way with me.'

Honey leaned forward, laughing until tears streamed. 'Very funny, Romeo. I have work tomorrow and God knows what time you'll get me home if you follow a freaking bus through its entire route. Tasha will give birth to an elephant, me having no respect for the work week. Fuck it, it does sound like fun. Let's go, Mr Elliott!'

Fourteen

April 2016

Ashley was once again preoccupied, Honey thought as she watched him from the passenger seat of his car. His mouth was moving silently, talking to himself as he drove. He pulled up outside Zeez on Kensington High Street.

'Quick,' he hurried her. 'There're cameras around like crazy, I don't need no eighty quid ticket for parking for a second. I'll pick you up around 4pm you say?'

Honey jumped out hurriedly. 'Yes. Thanks,' she said gratefully. Her car wasn't working and he had been picking her up and dropping her off wherever she needed to be. It made it look even more convincing to Natasha.

Honey was both proud and impressed with Fatty. She'd passed her management diploma and had made great improvements in Zeez while Fredrick was near to completing his Masters.

Fatty breezed out of her office, her face breaking into a smile at the sight of her friend. She gave a big wave. 'I'm coming, just have to finish off an order and explain this month's finances to Freddy's Dad. Za's back from America—she's through there.'

Honey walked along the narrow passage leading to the office at the back of the restaurant. Zhara was there, fiddling with the Wi-Fi. She looked up as Honey entered and squealed. In no time her long arms pulled Honey in, smothering her with kisses to her cheek. Honey laughed and held on to her friend.

'What's this I'm hearing about you and Ash? That shit still going on after nearly a whole year? What's really going on, Hon?'

Honey sat down at the desk in the small office and adjusted the keyboard in front of her unnecessarily. Zhara sat down opposite.

'Listen,' Honey leaned forward in Zhara's direction. 'It's only been seven months. Stop trying to make something out of this. It's a plan and it's going to plan.'

Fatty came into the office smiling, a bottle of wine and three wine goblets in her hand. 'My favourite people!' she said with arms outstretched.

'Take a seat,' Zhara pointed to the chair, 'Honey was about to tell me about this plan she has with Ash.'

Honey looked sharply at Zhara as Fatty opened the bottle and filled the goblets one by one.

'What plan? How comes I didn't know about this plan?' Fatty lifted her drink. 'To whatever we want to make of life,' she toasted. 'May we always be friends. Now, Hon, what plan?'

'The plan remains the same. Ash and I are pretending to

date so Tasha stops trying to hook me up with her friends' sons.'

Fatty looked at Zhara, puzzled. 'That's old news.'

'Yeah, I know,' Zhara sipped her drink, 'but why's it lasting so long? How comes Ash been going along with this for so long? Has he had your cherry?'

Honey sighed. 'Ashley Elliott, fuck me? Are you sick?'

Zhara dug deeper. 'Then why are you two carrying this thing on for so long? It doesn't make sense, unless you're really into each other and want to keep it a secret.'

'Are you serious?' Honey fumed.

'He ever kissed you?' Zhara sprang accusatorily.

Honey blushed. They saw it.

'Yes!' Zhara laughed. 'I knew it! I knew it!'

'Hon, you kissed Ash?' Fatty asked incredulously. She hadn't seen this coming.

'When I was a bit tipsy, I allowed him to kiss me. I guess I was a bit curious, you know; he's charming but a bit distant. Nothing happened. He was quite the *gentleman* and I woke up fully dressed and no sign of being fucked.'

'What the fuck! He's in love with you,' Fatty said in amazement.

'He isn't in love with me.' Honey said with assertion to drown out the loud beating of her heart.

'Were you disappointed that he didn't fuck you?' Zhara asked.

Honey squirmed. 'Hell no! I was glad.'

Zhara looked wistful. 'I wish it was me Ash wants. I'd have

given him it a long time ago. It's so not fair, the shit life dishes out.'

'You can have him, Za,' Honey offered, insincerely.

'It's not that simple, Hon. To have a man, he's got to want you, and Ash don't want me... he don't want any girl it seems, except you.'

Honey laughed. 'Are you crazy? It's just a game for him, he's still trying to get me between the sheets.'

'No, Ash must feel something more for you, Hon, or he wouldn't go along with that stupid plan. Bethany broke his heart over two years ago and no other woman has been able to get his attention since,' Zhara finished with a knowing nod.

'He feels more than something,' Fatty said, forehead creased in thought. 'Though I'm not sure if he understands his feelings. Ash is illusive. He don't talk much about his family. I know his dad ran off with some young girl back in the days. It did his mum's head in and she was put in a loony house, but Ash don't talk about that stuff.'

Honey looked taken aback. 'Wow! I didn't know that. Who did he grow up with?' she asked Fatty.

'Mostly his Aunt, I think. He's done well though.'

That he had, Honey thought to herself, softening to the warmth she couldn't help but feel towards him. 'And his little sister? Who does she live with?'

'His Aunt, but I know he used to take care of her. Ash won't talk about that side of him for whatever reason. It's a sore point. His father running off when his moms was pregnant with his little sister, that stinks—must give a young boy issues.'

Honey could see that. 'That would destroy anyone, being left alone with a baby.'

'If you can't get them at the abortion stage, there's always adoption. Now can we change the subject? I have a problem,' Zhara announced.

Fatty rolled her eyes. 'What now?'

'My Dad is trying to entice me back home... with the promise of big monies, my ladies. He says if I go home to visit my Grandma in Somalia before she dies, he'll give me enough to buy a flat anywhere in London,' Zhara enthused.

'Za, you know your Dad only wants to marry you off to calm you down. You said he thinks you living with your white British moms is a bad influence. He's always getting your brothers to watch you. If you go back to Somalia with him, I bet he's got a husband-cousin-uncle there waiting for you.'

Zhara looked horrified. 'You know, he is crafty like that.' The more the thought went around in her head, the more it made sense. She was his only daughter, 'illegitimate' though she may be; born to a white British woman he had an affair with. Her father lived with his Somali wife and five sons, his youngest just five months older than her.

'He's always trying to tempt me with money and gifts, all to get me on a plane.'

'Za, take the freaking gifts and the money and hit Florida, that's what I'd do. Why do I always have to be solving your problems! And Hon,' Fatty turned to her. 'Just make sure you know what you're doing. Kissing Ash tells me you're falling—you're not the kind of girl to kiss a guy if he means nothing.'

*

The sky had remained listless all day. White bleached and dreary, like a tarpaulin had been pulled across its vastness. When Ashley picked her up, she watched him with different eyes. She had not given much thought to his life, how he lived when he wasn't the showy business man running a club. Now she wanted to know more about the other side of his life, her curiosity rising with each thought.

She started thinking about his childhood and wondered what the real story was. She wondered about his ability to love. What did it do to him, his father leaving his mother? Did this Bethany alter his views on women in any way? What did he fear? He drove in silence, intense thoughts settled on his face.

'You okay, Ashley?' she asked.

He kept driving and shrugged. 'Not been feeling too good. Hot and cold sweats, headache. I must have picked up some mother-fucker bug.'

'You need to take more care of your health and spend time in your house instead of in your studio and the clubs.'

'My studio and my clubs are my bread and butter; I don't work, I don't get paid.'

'Dame and your staff can manage things. I mean, I don't know too much about the running of your businesses, but surely they're trained?'

'Look, Hon-Hon, you want to drive me home and take the car? I'm not feeling too good.' He pulled over suddenly and opened his door.

Honey slid over into the driver's seat, adjusting it to fit her legs. When Ashley got in the passenger seat, he altered the position so that he was laying back. She liked that he trusted her to drive his precious Porsche.

'I feel like shit.' He tightened his jacket around him, shivering.

Honey glanced at him briefly. 'You don't look good.' She touched his forehead with the back of her hand. 'You got any flu medicine at home? You've got a temperature.'

'No. My medicine is weed, it cures everything.'

'Well you smoke it all the time so how on earth did you even get sick if that's the case?' She smiled slyly.

He ignored her, closing his eyes and cursing.

The flat was cool with the familiar smell of leather and marijuana. Ashley immediately took off his jacket and started to undress, heading straight for the bedroom.

'You want me to make you some chicken soup? I'll put lots of hot pepper in it so you sweat out that virus.'

He didn't answer and she went into the kitchen and started preparing. It surprised her that his fridge was stacked with healthy options: pineapple, mangoes and kiwi, ready packed; spinach, lettuce, tomatoes, carrots, aubergines, yams, sweet potatoes and peppers. She wondered how he got time to cook. In the freezer compartment, she found two frozen fish heads but no chicken, so she went about making fish tea, chopping onions, green and red peppers, and garlic to add to the boiling fish heads; with thyme, salt and hot pepper to taste. By the time she went into the bedroom, Ashley was silently sleeping, wrapped snug in the duvet and sweating heavily. She placed the bowl of soup on the bedside table and sat on the bed, using a towel to gently wipe his face.

'Ashley, wake up and drink at least five spoons of this fish soup,' she said, shaking him. He opened his eyes and struggled to prop himself up. She blew to cool the liquid on the spoon before placing it to his lips. Ashley sipped and swallowed, then kept his mouth open for more until the bowl had finished.

He laid back and wrapped himself once more in the duvet. 'Can you call Dame and tell him to cover for me? I'll call him later.'

Honey nodded.

'Thanks, Hon-Hon, that soup was delicious,' he smiled, lopsided, 'and so are you. Wish I had some energy.' His eyes fought to stay open, but she watched as sleep made him floppy, taking him deeper into a mysterious world of dreams that made him mumble incoherently, twisting and turning. She called her manager, mimicking all of Ashley's symptoms, and had no qualms in doing so. It was three more days before he felt well enough to get out of bed. Dame popped around, dressed, as usual, in tight denim jeans and pink tee.

'Ash, you don't look that sick to me—looks like you've been living the life of Riley, with your own personal maid and chef, by the looks of things.' Dame leaned back on the soft, black leather sofa and crossed his legs. He smiled teasingly at

Honey.

Ashley was sat on the single sofa, donned in pyjamas, the TV remote in his hand as he surfed through channels.

Honey responded, 'You should have seen him. He only got up to use the toilet and shower. He even lost his taste for weed.' Dame looked unconvinced. 'That won't last. No doubt he was enjoying the nursing and pampering,' he grinned mischievously.

'Dame, what's the story, man? Not enough work for you?' Ashley asked, without taking his eyes off the TV screen.

'Taking a lunch break, boss, as is permitted by some EU employment law somewhere. I figured you may miss my face.' He patted the sofa, inviting Honey to sit beside him. She smiled and plopped herself down.

'Has this pretend relationship turned real?' Dame pointed theatrically towards Ashley who had his back to him and was still focused on the TV. 'I mean, you were defending his fake illness with passion there.' He winked.

Honey's eyes widened; she wasn't expecting Dame to come so direct.

Ashley turned around, his face void of any humour. Three days without eating had hollowed his cheeks and left dark circles under his eyes. 'You've overstayed your welcome.'

Dame stood up, sniggering. 'No prob boss, I was going anyway. Bye Hon,' he blew Honey a kiss, gave a brief salute to Ashley and then he was gone.

Honey busied herself cleaning up the kitchen before she joined Ashley in the lounge. She puffed up the cushions and seated herself. 'I'll go home tomorrow now you're much better, Tasha hasn't stopped texting. This makes us look real.'

Ashley smiled. 'Thanks. You didn't have to help me out like that, yeah. I appreciate it.'

'You'd better.' She returned his smile.

'If you like, I can show you just how much I appreciate you.' It was suggestive, the sexy smile that stretched his lips, the twinkle in his eyes, the tip of his tongue that played with his teeth. She laughed.

'You've had a lot of missed calls over the past few days. I'm pretty sure Marla would appreciate a call.'

'Yes, she would.' His face softened. 'Marla is my account-ant, nothing more. The property I'm interested in must have come through. Just so you know, you're all that fills my head... this pretend relationship of ours.'

After Honey had left, Ashley became aware of how quiet his flat was without her noises floating around. There was still a hint of her perfume and he closed his eyes to remember how she cooled the spoonfuls of soup before placing them to his mouth. How the softness of her hand on his face, his forehead, his neck, as she checked his temperature made his body react. There were times when he thought she had feelings for him, but he was never really sure because of her brand of sarcasm. He would have liked it if she had shown even a little jealousy over Marla. His phone rang; It was Marla.

'S'up, girl.'

'Ash! I've been calling you for days. Dame says you were laid up with the flu. Bethany called, pouring her heart out about how sorry she is, how she misses you and wants me to put in a good word for her—'

'Bethany made her choice when she jumped in bed with Bruce. Any news on my offer on the Fairfield Village property?'

Fifteen

Ashley looked in the mirror and wondered if he was going mad. Was his mother's manic-depressive gene rearing its head in him? God, he hoped not. But what else could describe the way Honey was making him feel? He burned for her twenty-four hours a day. On awakening in the mornings, even before he could open his eyes, she filled him, her face coming together like a jigsaw. Her eyes, her lips, her teeth, her sweet pink tongue, her hair. She had become the colours in his life. He loved and hated the thought equally. Especially because she was so cool towards him. It did his head in that he couldn't decode her like other women. And he would have gone on thinking and wondering about her had he not looked down to see his phone was vibrating, an unknown number on the screen.

'Talk.' Ashley answered all unknown calls in that manner. This was his personal number.

'Mr Elliott? Ashley Elliott?'

'Who's this?'

'I'm calling from Ealing Hospital.'

Ashley was instantly anxious. 'Yes, I'm Ashley Elliott.

What's wrong? What's going on?'

The hesitation on the other end of the phone was infuriating and in that nano second, he willed his mind to freeze, to block out anything that would send him back to hell.

'Your mother is here, and I think you should come. She's on St Matthew's Ward.'

Ashley dressed, pulling on Nike tracksuit bottoms and a plain white tee shirt. St Matthew's Ward was the mental wellness section of Ealing Hospital. He knew it well. For most of his school years, he had to visit his mother in that building. When he arrived, Mrs Reece, the manager of Barns House where his mother lived, was also there with a wide friendly smile that could not hide the concerns she felt. She was small, pink and round, and oozed the maternal energy that grief and uncertainty hungered for. She held out a familiar hand and Ashley held on. She was warm. She led him to sit down.

'I'm so sorry, Ashley,' she spoke with a Scottish brogue, 'your mother made another attempt on her life. She was on cooking duties with Sally in room 2, and was just supposed to peel the potatoes. But she tried to-to cut her throat and her wrists with the potato peeler. She did some bad damage, but she will be alright, physically.'

This was not a strange place to be for Ashley. The words were normal, had been for many years. His mother wanting to end her life, and why? Because his father left her for another woman, a much younger woman. Left her when she was pregnant and she could never find herself again.

'I hate him, Mrs Reece, I hate him. He's the reason she

wants to end it all. I wish I could make her happy. Why won't she let me?'

'You do make her happy, Ashley. You're the only one who does. You can't change what your father did, and it's not your fault. You have been your mother's rock and you should be proud of yourself. Your mother needs to give herself permission to be happy; you can't make that happen on your own.'

'Can I see her?' he asked gloomily.

'Yes, but she's been sedated and will be out for the night. Follow me.'

His mother was in a room by herself. A drab, white walled room with a sink and a tiny window. She looked peaceful, sleeping like she had no care in the world. He held back the urge to gather her into his arms and cradle her, like he remembered her arms cradling him when life was good and happy, before Marley was born. Her neck had been bandaged, as were both wrists. Ashley squeezed his eyes tight to avert the tears.

'You should go home now and get yourself some rest,' Mrs Reece spoke softly.

Ashley tried calling Nathan, his elder brother in America; he needed to talk to him, to someone, to ease the grief that was creeping around him. The answer phone kicked in and he just left a message saying, "Call me." He drove at breakneck speed to his Auntie Dawn's house, where Marley lived. He broke yellow and red lights, ignored car horns and finger gestures of annoyed motorists. He wanted to talk. He wanted to tell his Auntie Dawn that her big sister had tried to kill herself again.

Auntie Dawn lived in a two bedroom house in Fulham,

at the mouth of the notorious Bleakhead council Estate where top range BMW's, Audie's and Lexus' could be seen parked. He had lived here too, when his mother was yet again unable to care for him and Marley. He walked up to the door and was soon ringing the doorbell.

Auntie Dawn was a larger version of his mother. They both had alabaster skin, blue eyes and brown curly hair. Both grew up with strict catholic parents, lashings of Sunday school and bible classes. Auntie Dawn raised two children alone, both now happily married. He often wondered why his mother couldn't have done the same.

The flat remained like his Aunt, he thought, as he followed behind her into the living room, warm and comfortable, always smelling of something just baked, fried or boiled. The wall colours were always the same, even when re-painted it reverted back to its original colours: brown kitchen, yellow living room, pink toilet and bathroom, and white bedrooms, always white. Ashley was relieved to see Marley was home, sitting on the sofa, her head stuck in a book. He was proud of the way she took her education seriously, proud of the way she had come through despite having such a disruptive life, knowing her mother didn't love or care for her.

'Mom's in St Matthew's, Auntie Dawn,' Ashley spoke hurriedly.

'Again,' Marley huffed, not looking up from her book.

'Yes,' Ashley snapped. 'She tried to cut her throat and slash her wrists,' he said, almost pleading, hoping maybe that he could get his Aunt and sister to show that they cared.

Love Again

'I just wish she would get herself together,' Auntie Dawn sighed, sitting down and picking up a copy of Home and Gardening. 'You must stop taking it all on board, Ash. Your childhood has been spent worrying about your mother, and her problems are self-inflicted. A waste of a life if you ask me.'

Ashley had heard this unfinished story his entire childhood. Auntie Dawn's empathy for her older sister had left many years ago. He couldn't stay here, not listening to his sister and aunt's total disregard for his mother's plight.

'I'll see you guys later,' he turned and headed out the door, angry and grieved.

Auntie Dawn called after him. 'Ash, come on. You can't do any more than what you've been doing. Doreen has to do the rest and she just doesn't want to. I love my sister too, but I'm not going to let her—'

Ashley slammed the front door and took the stairs to his car. He sat for a long moment just breathing and thinking about his mother and her death wish. He wanted to talk. He needed to talk. He phoned Honey.

'Are you busy? Can I see you... please, Honey? I—I—'

'Ashley? What's wrong? Where are you?'

'In Fulham, just visited my Aunt and sister. I just want to talk. My Moms, she's—she's—'

'I'll meet you at your house in an hour,' she told him.

When Honey rang his doorbell, he had been home just fifteen minutes and was on his second glass of Grey Goose and Red Bull. He opened the door, his eyes cloudy with the pain of his mother's suffering. The feeling of hopelessness that he could do nothing to ease her anguish increased his anger towards his father. He gave a small, sad smile. Honey sat cautiously opposite him, across the coffee table.

'What's wrong with your mother?' she asked, breaking the silence on seeing that Ashley sat motionless and silent, staring miserably ahead for what seemed like an age without any intention to speak.

'She's sick. I thought she might die, but the doctor says she'll be fine. She tried to slit her throat, slashed both her wrists too. I mean, she meant to kill herself. She's tried before you know, many times. I came home once and found her head in the oven with the gas on. I was twelve and so scared. I've been trying to save her since... but—but I can't and it hurts that I can't make her happy. I'm scared she'll eventually—'

Honey stood up and walked around the coffee table to sit close to him. She took his hand and held it. 'It's okay to be scared.'

'I don't want her to die, Hon-Hon. I don't want my Moms gone. I want her to be happy again, even if it's just for one day. I want to see her smile, hear her real laugh again. I haven't heard any of that since I was ten years old and I dream about it all the time... her laughter, her being herself again.' He held on to a sob, breathed it away, annoyed with himself now that he had even called Honey.

Honey's arms were around his neck and he could hear the warmth and softness in her voice filling his ears, smell the warm vanilla zest of her fragrance and, despite the grief that gripped him, his body was reacting to her closeness, to the softness of her, the breeze from her hair. Before he knew it, her lips had taken his and she was kissing him. Honey was kissing him in the way that said she wanted it all. He pulled away from her, afraid. Her eyes were deep with a desire that froze him. What did she expect? She came at him again, her hungry lips too delicious to resist. She was unbuttoning his shirt, his trousers, and all the time her lips were there, on offer, causing his body to surrender, enveloped by the sweetest of sensations, perhaps, love, he thought. He had never felt desire so deep, but had doubts about the aftermath.

'Hon-Hon, don't. You don't know what you're doing—' he held her close but still. He was afraid.

'Ashley, take me. I know exactly what I'm doing, so take me, and take me now.' She licked his neck, her tongue travelling around his ear, settling to nibble on his lobe.

He groaned. 'Are we pretending? Hon, please, please, let's think about this—' her kisses were addictive, and despite his protests he was responding and removing her clothing, his hands multitasking, roaming her body and simultaneously removing his own clothes.

'I don't need to. I want you. I want you,' she began helping him to completely remove his shirt and trouser.

'You're gonna hate me in the morning. You're going to blame me, you're going to hate me forever.'

'I won't. I want you, now, this moment. I want you. Nothing else matters right now.'

'Has hell frozen over?'

'Hell doesn't exist, now shut up and make me yours.'

Rasheda Ashanti Malcolm

It wasn't until morning, when the sorry arse sun had finally poked its shy head through the white, puffy clouds, that he studied the body that had taken him into another dimension. Her small breasts, chocolate nipples still erect, slim toned body. And she had the audacity to be sleeping peacefully, her full, luscious lips slightly parted, allowing the soft noise of sleep to escape, her lashes curled, resting on her rounded cheeks, and her brown-black hair a halo on the pillow. He was never more in love than this moment. Bethany couldn't compare to Honey Elizabeth Fontaine.

Sixteen

April 2016

What a perfect time for rain, Honey thought as she sat on her bedroom window ledge looking out across the common, engrossed in thoughts that made her blush, squirm, and reflect. The rain was pelting down, and for the people walking across the green with their umbrellas up, it was a struggle against the wind that accompanied the shower. It was Saturday, so shoppers, motorists and pedestrians just wanted to go home or enjoy their weekend in the pubs and clubs. Natasha was frying fish and chips for dinner, a regular on Saturdays, and its smell was drifting into Honey's room despite the closed door. A whole month had passed since she slept with Ashley and she hadn't seen him since. She'd been avoiding him. Embarrassment was always close. He called and she spoke as normally as she could, but it was hard. Hard because her feelings for him went deeper than she wanted them to. She feared that it was more than a crush, that she already loved him, but she wasn't enjoying it and would certainly not pursue it past what it was. Fatty and Zhara called as well, and she had to be mindful of her words because they could read her well. Making up her mind, she decided she would call off the whole trick on Natasha. This way she and Ashley could return to their normal life.

Honey looked at her watch to see it was still only 4:20pm and there was no ease up from the internal turmoil. She'd picked at her fish and chips before heading back to her room. She was close to despair when Fatty and Zhara opened her bedroom door.

'Why you hiding away and what's the glum face for?' Fatty entered first, flopping down on the bed beside her. Zhara followed, sandwiching Honey between them.

'And why's the telly on without the volume?' Zhara picked up the remote. 'Are you heart-broken about something, Hon?'

Honey had to think fast, but she was so overjoyed at seeing her friends at such a time of total angst, that the relief lifted the lid on her happiness and she started laughing.

'That's better.' Fatty pushed against her affectionately. 'Freddy gave me the afternoon off and I thought I'd spend it with you. Any update on the Ash situation?' she laughed.

'Forget that. Listen you guys, my Dad has offered my mother 20K if she lets him take me to Somalia—she says it would be good for me to visit to meet my grandparents and that the money would help us both.'

'Shit!' Fatty's hands cupped her opened jaws. 'Your arse is in for a marriage.'

Honey was glad for the distraction from the gnawing thoughts of Ashley. Her eyes registered the TV, then Zhara's face, etched with a frown.

'I think Fatty's right,' Honey said, clearing her throat and wishing she could clear Ashley just as easily. 'That's the trick families play, pretending they're taking you to visit relatives when they have your life planned for you.'

'Well, I'm not going. I told my mum, but the money's got her interest and she keeps telling me that I'd only stay two weeks and come back.' Zhara folded her arms.

'You're right to forget that shit or you'd find yourself stuck in some kitchen tied to a fucking cooker. So, Hon,' Fatty smiled teasingly. 'What's the update with Ash? I wish you would finish that crap with Ash and just think about getting serious with someone. Maybe you can even give one of Tasha's intros a chance. Freddy's brought so much love into my life; I just want you and Za to have that as well.'

'That would be nice,' Zhara purred. 'At the end of the day you can't help thinking about that perfect man for you, and how your lives will look entwined—'

'Are you serious, Fats? You want me to consider Tasha's intros?' Honey looked disgusted.

'I would,' Zhara piped in. 'Tasha only wants rich, successful guys who are going places for you... I'd give it a chance. That joke thing with Ash has had its run. I don't think for one minute that Tasha really believes it's real, that's why she won't let up. And anyway, I don't feel Ash will love or trust another woman after what Bethany did.'

Zhara couldn't know the turbulence her words caused her friend's heart. The thought that he would never trust or love her after what he and she shared; the way he looked at her as they made love, the things he did to her body and mind—after all that he would hold her responsible for another woman's action? Her heart silently splintered.

✻

Honey's open plan office in Lyric Square was on the third floor, and she shared it with twenty-one other colleagues. Fenelle Communications broadcasted their daily radio shows on FM and Online, and Honey was the assistant script manager, a job she couldn't see herself doing as a career. Her degree had been in Media and Marketing and her favourite medium was print. Lately she had taken to wanting to have her own publishing company, or working more in operations, where she could develop her creative skills making programmes.

The pale-yellow walls, intersected by huge windows and a glass door to the office, pretty much reflected the lack of imagination by Fenelle Communication management, as far as Honey was concerned. Every time she had tried to make an input at management meetings, teased them to think outside of the box, it always ended the same. The MD thought it was a good idea but... and that *but* was always left unexplained. She was frustrated in her job at the least. She had big dreams, big wonderful dreams that she enjoyed manoeuvring through in the quiet-lonely space of her bedroom. There she was director and producer of a masterpiece—her life and what she would make of it.

'Penny for them.' Honey tore her eyes reluctantly from

looking out of the window towards the busy and leisurely movements of the people. She was trying to make time move faster by zoning out and away. Her colleague, Tamara, bubbly brunette and pretty green eyes, stood in front of her desk, smiling.

'You okay, Honey? For the past few weeks you've not been yourself.'

Honey pulled for her ready-made smile that said 'everything is fine' and nodded. 'I was thinking about moving out of my parents—'

'Wow, can you afford it?' Tamara asked, leaning forward.

'Not exactly. Not on what I make. I'm in love with the idea of running my own business, a publishing company.'

'Something made you unhappy at home or here at work?'

Tamara was a nice enough girl, but Honey suddenly felt invaded. She didn't want to talk about what was making her unhappy. Was it so obvious, she thought?

'No,' Honey said softly, 'but there comes a time when you got to fly the nest, move out on your own.'

'I know the feeling,' Tamara confessed. 'We're living with Ray's parents but there's no way for at least another five to six years before we can afford our own place.'

Tamara's conversation and her constant disruption of Honey's working day made things speed up, and before she knew it, the magical 5pm had arrived and Honey had made a habit of quitting right on time, trying to beat the rush of work mates with the same intentions.

It was like de ja vu as she walked out into the car park.

There perched on her car, with his lean, fine athletic body that she now knew intimately, was Ashley, looking like the Adonis from her dreams, but the cheeky smile was accompanied by a trace of uncertainty.

'I told you, didn't I? Told you you'd hate me.' Ashley's directness knocked her and it took a few seconds for her to recover, to stop her insides from shaking and her arms from sliding around his neck and engulfing his lips with hers. Hate him? He had no idea. God, she burned for him.

'I don't hate you,' she looked around, conscious of anyone she knew who could overhear this conversation.

'Then why are you avoiding me?'

She looked helplessly at him, feeling the love she felt would frighten him. If he was so in love with this Bethany who broke his heart, maybe he would never love again. She couldn't take the chance and tell him how she really felt about him.

'Look,' he told her, 'we can forget about, you know, our bedroom activity. I just don't want you avoiding me like this. I got used to you and I want you around me, if that makes any sense.'

'I don't think that would work. I overstepped the mark in our agreement. I shouldn't have, but at the time I felt you were... I felt the need to have you for whatever crazy reason. But now, in the light of day I need to apologise because it shouldn't have happened. I was wrong.'

Ashley watched her steadily, his eyes penetrative and still, despite her rapid eye movements. He really couldn't understand her way of thinking, how she could be so dismissive of him. It hurt. Reaching for a strand of her hair, he wound it around his finger. 'For what it's worth, I had a good time with you. I regret nothing.'

Moving his finger from her hair, she sighed. 'I regret everything.' She looked away because if he held on to her eyes any longer, he would surely see the dishonesty in her words.

Seventeen

June 2016

Ashley hung up the phone and leaned back in his chair. He was at the office in the club, a small room with blank walls, a desk, two chairs and a filing cabinet, a place he spent little time in. His main office was at A One Studio, which had all the comforts a wealthy and successful boss could want. It even housed a sleeping quarter, should he want to entertain, because, apart from Honey Elizabeth Fontaine, he had never taken any woman back to his flat. Not even Bethany. He always stayed at hers.

As he walked out into the bar area of the club, he greeted the regular day time punters playing pool and who he knew would be there until the club closed at 2am, supporting the bar and his profits all the way to the bank. Even as they smiled and shook his hand, he could feel the emptiness in their lives, and was glad he had chosen a different path, and persisted.

Why did she have to be like this? He pondered for the umpteenth time. Now she called the whole thing off and he would have no excuse to see her again. She didn't want to see him again, which hurt like hell. For a while there, he thought something was growing between them. Bethany was long out of his mind, and he didn't trust to love again, until Honey, but without her presence to gauge this feeling, he would never know. *God, she was difficult!*

When his phone rang and he answered it, it was Marley, reminding him that her prom was coming up and he should start thinking about her dress, go shopping with her to choose it and get it out the way. He couldn't think of anything less appealing and told her as much. Then he wondered if he could use this as an excuse to get in contact with Honey. He called her immediately after Marley, and she answered in that hesitant way she developed since their sleeping together. He wished he could convey how different it had been with her, how lying with her had brought him to a new and different dimension and he wanted more.

'Ashley...'

'Hon-Hon, how you been?'

'Fine, thank you.'

'You have to be so fucking formal? Was it that bad for you?'

Honey smiled. He broke the ice and she suddenly realised the weight of carrying around this unrequited love. She needed to put it down and get on with life. She needed to learn how to un-love him without his or anyone else's knowledge.

'Sorry, the job can sometimes stick in my head, I get all absorbed,' she lied.

'You can always come and work for me.' She heard his

laugh and imagined his lips spreading to reveal his smooth, white teeth. 'I need your help, girl. Marley needs a prom gown and wants some help, not from me, so I thought maybe you could go shopping with her? You know, give some girly advice about hair and make-up and all that stuff.'

Honey found herself feeling flattered that he trusted her to take his little sister shopping. He hadn't been too open about his life outside of the club, so she felt honoured.

'I'll take her. When?'

Ashley punched a celebratory fist in the air. He would spend some time with Honey again. Even if he would not hold her in his arms or kiss her lips, he would be able to smell her subtle perfume, see her face and at the least, curl her hair around his finger.

'Sunday would be cool—she has a Saturday job.'

*

Honey was at a loose end that Saturday afternoon when her mother surprised her with a ticket to the Alicia Keys concert at the Hammersmith Odeon. It would mean Honey going along with Natasha and her friends, but that was bearable if it meant seeing her idol, Alicia.

Honey made great efforts with her appearance due to the sudden surge in happiness the phone call from Ashley had sparked. It meant a lot that he called her, it meant he was thinking about her—and her heart knew no greater joy. Her mother helped her do her hair, wash, blow dry and then straightened from its curls, resting down her back. She applied her makeup light, smoky eyes and cherry red lipstick. Her off the shoulder red dress fitted her slim body, accentuating her in the right places, and, looking in the mirror, she smiled at the beauty staring back at her.

The Hammersmith Odeon already had a crowd, even though Natasha had the good sense to have the taxi drop them off an hour and a half before the doors were due to open. Standing in the queue, they were joined by Natasha's friend, Ruby, and a handsome young man, who was immediately introduced to Honey as Ruby's Banker nephew, Kevin, which made Honey clock the real reason her ticket was bought. She viewed her mother sternly but was able to deliver a polite greeting to the tall, handsome young man who returned her smile with a warmth she wasn't anticipating.

'Your mother said you were beautiful, I thought it was just a mother's boast... but you are,' Kevin finished softly. With his height and build, not to mention the deep brown eyes and smiling full lips, he could pass for one of those American footballers, Honey thought, looking a bit like the notorious OJ Simpson when he was younger.

'Thank you,' she smiled, 'you're not bad yourself.'

Natasha hurried ahead, linking her arm through Ruby's, happy that Honey seemed to like Kevin.

'Your mother says you're a big fan of Alicia. Me too,' he continued, with his magic laced smile.

'Don't believe everything my mother tells you about me,' she warned, half serious.

'That's not my style. I prefer to make my own judgement about a person.'

It wasn't long before they were on their feet, singing and swaying to Alicia Keys' greatest hits, songs that painted the story of a woman's love, her broken heart, her unbroken spirit. Honey had always been intrigued that beautiful people, someone as beautiful as Alicia, had encountered such torment in love that she could write those songs.

'Can we lunch, or dinner, sometime?' Kevin asked after the standing ovation, as people began to gather bags and jackets.

Honey took a good look at him, until he began to blush. 'I'm sorry. I was staring. Of course we can have lunch or dinner, your preference.'

'I'd rather it be yours. Why were you staring at me like that?'

She shrugged. 'Just hoping my mother didn't put you up to asking me out—'

'When you get to know me better,' he cut her short with a gentle smile, 'you'll know that no-one can put me up to anything. The moment I saw you I was interested, in the most respectful way.'

She had been staring at Kevin to compare him to Ashley, to see if there was anything in him that reminded her of him. She was disappointed, and once again annoyed with herself.

He and Ruby drove Honey and Natasha home. All the way to Ealing he joked and Honey laughed and Natasha was ecstatic. When Kevin drove around the green and into the cul-de-sac, it was after 2am and he got out of the car quickly to run to the passenger side to open the door for Honey, taking her hand. She smiled.

'So, here's my number,' he gave her a card, 'call me or text me when you're ready for that lunch or dinner.'

'Thanks. I had a lovely time, goodnight.' She gave him that stare again, he noticed, before following her mother into the house.

Natasha put an arm around Honey as they walked up the stairs. 'Isn't Kevin a darling? So handsome... and wealthy.' She squeezed Honey's shoulder.

'That's the only reason you bought me a ticket, so you can continue with your arranged marriage business. He seems nice enough but don't get any funny ideas.'

That was enough encouragement for Natasha; she was already hearing wedding bells. Before she slept, Honey took out Kevin's card and texted: *It's Honey, I finish work at 3pm on Friday, so could do a late lunch?* Kevin's response was almost immediate. *Friday's great. You have any favourite restaurants?*

Honey smiled. He scored points for being considerate enough to ask her opinion.

There's a great Caribbean restaurant in Mayfair. A bit of a drive, but it's worth it. Only problem will be the traffic around Hyde Park and maybe parking in the area. Again the response was instant.

I don't mind being stuck in traffic with you for hours if need be, then he put a blushing smiley emoji face. *And my friend's business is around that area, so we have parking.*

Honey snuggled under her duvet feeling relieved. Perhaps

Rasheda Ashanti Malcolm

Kevin could be the distraction she needed to keep her thoughts away from Ashley Elliott. It would be much easier meeting with Ashley under the guises of friendship if she had her own love interest. It was turning out that she missed him. *Not good*, she scolded herself. *Not good.*

✱

Ashley arrived Sunday morning earlier than he promised, 9am on the dot. It was Honey who kept him waiting, a whole twenty minutes before she was ready. The house smelt of home, with the fresh toasted and buttered bread, and the steaming coffee percolating. Aaron invited him to sit in the kitchen at the breakfast bar and wait for Honey. Natasha smirked in her usual way but he had started to accept that was her way of smiling.

'Honey's late because she came home after 1am last night. Her and Natasha went to see Alicia Keys at Hammersmith Odeon,' Aaron explained to Ashley.

Ashley nodded even though he had no idea that Honey had gone out last night. He spoke to her earlier that same day and she never mentioned anything about going out. But then it was not their habit to inform each other of things like that. He had already admitted to himself that he missed her, even if what they had had been pretend, as she so vocally made it clear. He missed her. Worse since their sexual encounter, which now seemed a world away.

'Oh, and Kevin and Ruby were there,' Natasha sat opposite

141

her husband at the breakfast bar and sipped her coffee, her conversation excluding Ashley. 'Kevin has a career in banking, he works for some hedge fund company and is doing quite well.'

Aaron knew where his wife was heading and shot her a warning look. As far as he knew, Honey and Ashley were still dating.

'He and Honey got on really well,' her eyes flipped briefly over Ashley before looking back to her husband. 'And they have so much in common.'

'Honey is a friendly girl, she gets on well with everyone,' Aaron laughed lightly, 'you sure you don't want any coffee or toast?' He offered the plate to Ashley who shook his head.

'Then let's listen to some news in the lounge and wait for Honey.' Ashley was thankful for that.

Honey looked tired, Ashley thought as they drove mostly in silence towards Fulham to pick up Marley. He was quiet because he now understood that smirk on Natasha's face; she had found someone to match Honey with. He was fuming, quietly.

This was the wettest June he could remember. The car's windscreen wiper criss-crossed to keep the screen clear of the downpour and Honey turned up the music to fill the silence. Ashley glanced at her sideways, quickly returning his eyes to the road. He turned the music down.

'You okay, Hon-Hon? Heard you had a great night out at Alicia.'

Honey laughed. 'Tasha told you, right?'

Rasheda Ashanti Malcolm

'No, it was your Dad. Natatrash just made sure I over-heard what she wanted me to hear.' His response was curt.

'Alicia was just out of this world, she sang all the favourites and some new stuff. She looked amazing,' Honey enthused, becoming animated.

'Well, I can see you really enjoyed yourself. Natatrash also said you had a lot in common with your date.'

Honey burst into laughter, real laughter, the first since realising she was in love with Ashley. Ashley sounded peeved about Kevin. It was far from an admission of any true feelings for her, but it felt good.

'It wasn't a date in that sense, but yes, Kevin was very interesting. I don't know enough about him to say we have a whole lot in common, but I know he's in banking—'

'Natatrash told me.' Ashley swerved into the outside lane and then signalled to return to middle lane. His stomach was twisting. He felt physically sick at the thought of her with anyone else. She had made it clear she had no interest in him and he accepted that. Yet at home, in the stillness of night, lying in his bed he could still feel her body against him, under him, over him, as though she had left a layer of herself stuck to him. His body always reacted.

'This is a terrible day to shop, with all this rain. I'll take Marley to the little boutique off Oxford Street. They sell special occasion dresses, I'm sure she'll find something there.' Honey was cheerful. She felt lifted from her low mood of the past months. Kevin had given her the confidence to face Ashley, without fearing Ashley would read her love.

143

The rain had eased to a drizzle as the car came to a halt on a street of terraced houses, and Honey saw the curtain of the red house move, and then the door opened and a slender teenage girl, dressed in black leggings stood balancing perfectly on one leg.

'Let's go in and say hi to my Auntie Dawn, she won't take kindly if we don't.'

Honey was hugely surprised and even more intrigued about meeting a member of Ashley's family, and those butter-flies were back in her stomach. He took her hand and led her to the door. She couldn't stop her heart from cartwheeling, recalling how his hand had felt moving over her skin.

The young girl on one leg jumped at Ashley and he had to release Honey's hand to catch her, lifting her off the door-step. She wrapped her slim arms around his neck and he hugged her tightly. When he put her down Honey could see aspects of Ashley in the contours of her face, only with darker complexion.

'Marley, this is Honey. Hon-Hon, this is my baby sis, Marley.' He sounded so proud and when his sister looked up at him with admiration illuminating her face, Honey was touched.

'Nice to meet you, Marley,' Honey placed her cheek against the young girl's.

'Nice meeting you too,' Marley said, tilting her head to one side, just like her brother did before he had some comment to make. 'You look just like Halle Berry.'

Honey gave Marley a wide smile and a hug. 'I can see you

and I will get on well with compliments like that.'

Marley's hand went around Honey's waist as she walked her into a small living room, big enough only for the three-seat sofa and a coffee table, comfortably. The television was fitted to the yellow wall next to what could be described as a masterpiece: a huge glass clock with imitation diamond studs signifying the numbers on the face.

Auntie Dawn stood up. Tall and curvy, with creases under her eyes and around her mouth, she was dressed in trendy jeans and a tie-dye tee shirt.

'And who do we have here?' She grabbed her glasses from off the coffee table and hurriedly put them on, taking a step to meet Honey.

'Auntie, this is Honey. She's going to help Marley shop for her prom dress.'

Auntie Dawn took Honey's hand in her warm, soft ones and pulled her closer, peering at her in wonder. 'I'm so glad to meet Ashley's girlfriend—'

'We're just friends, Auntie,' Honey said, holding her hand in a warm clasp.

'Yes, just friends,' Ashley chirped. 'Honey has a boyfriend, Kevin,' he smiled wickedly. 'He's in banking.'

Auntie Dawn's head swung amusingly from Ashley to Honey, taking in the looks of annoyance passing between them before bursting into laughter.

'Well it doesn't matter, as long as you both know you're friends,' she smiled mischievously.

It was easier than Honey thought, helping Marley pick out

a prom dress. She was so thrilled by them all she had Honey choose, and within the hour they returned to the car where Ashley had sat parked, waiting solemnly, Honey noted.

'Can we have a Mickey D?' Marley asked. 'We finished shopping earlier, so why not?' She ended with a whine to her voice.

'I thought you were into healthy eating.' Ashley's mood was quiet.

'I know Poochie's,' Marley sprung up and down on the back seat. 'It's like a posh Mickey D with healthy options. I know it, my friend's godmother takes her there. Can we go Ash, please?'

'Auntie's got her roast chicken and potatoes ready for you and home-made bread, that's a healthy option.' He sighed.

Honey was puzzled by his melancholy mood.

Ashley was too wound up to eat. To think their night together meant so little to her that she could treat him so casually, start something with someone else, this Kevin. He unreasonably felt betrayed, fleetingly comparing her to Bethany. Would he ever find a woman who would only want him?

When he pulled up outside Auntie Dawn's house, Honey got out at the same time as Marley and smiled warmly at the young girl.

'It was nice meeting you, Marley.'

Marley threw her arms around Honey. 'Thanks so much for helping to choose my prom dress, it's absolute magic. Are you coming in for some of Auntie's roast chicken?'

Honey declined, shaking her head. 'No, I have to get home now, got some preparation to do for work. I'll see you soon.'

Pulling up in the cul-de-sac, Ashley switched off the engine and turned to her.

'Let's call a truce,' he offered his hand. She looked at the long fingers that had pleasured her and blushed at her private thoughts. 'I can't understand why you're hating on me like this, girl. I was the one who said we shouldn't, and now you hate me.'

Honey blinked. 'No, I don't hate you, Ashley. Of course, I don't hate you. A truce it is.' She opened the car door, keeping her eyes on his, wishing with all her heart she could tell him how she really felt.

Eighteen

Kevin invited Honey to a private viewing of his artist friend, who the Guardian newspaper had called an *emerging, contemporary, culturally explorative artistic talent.* Honey wasn't quite sure of what she was looking at when she saw his work, but she was artistically sensitive enough to show great awe and appreciation when nothing made sense, as it did with Hugo Patel's work. Hugo was a small, slim man, mixed Indian with his mother's clear blue eyes and father's brown skin, the frivolous charm of a Bollywood actor and the perfect white toothed smile to match.

'He's a busy man,' was all Honey could say to Kevin who had just introduced them, Hugo kissing her hand hurriedly before being whisked off by his agent to meet someone more important than them.

They were walking around the Tate Gallery, taking in the other exhibits. 'I'll introduce you to him properly another time, tonight is his night,' Kevin said apologetically, and Honey held back her tongue to ask why he thought Hugo needed another introduction.

Kevin suddenly came to a halt. 'Where do you want to eat? It's almost lunch time.'

Honey really didn't feel like eating. The queasy feelings that had been coming and going over the past few months were lingering today, and common sense told her she needed food.

'Rolly-Polly's in Streatham. I haven't been to south London in ages.' She wanted to be out of the West, admitting to herself that she didn't want anyone to see her with Kevin, who would relay it back to Ashley. *Stupid,* she cursed.

Honey and Kevin stood looking at his Range Rover, a stunning Blue.

'The front seats are heated, and they have lumbar support and memory seats,' he boasted, and Honey felt her heart deflate at such bragging and information download about a car.

'Let me drive,' she held out her hand for the key, pretending her attention had been momentarily grabbed by the adorable ginger haired identical twin boys, who just happened to be passing with their proud father. Honey noted Kevin's hesitation. She turned her head to look at him, her hand still held out.

Kevin broke into a smile. 'Okay,' he placed the key in her hand, squeezing gently. 'Anything for you.'

She drove relaxed and confident, loving the smooth, easy movement of the car, the comfort the seats offered and the surround sound system providing a gentle bed of music beneath their friendly talk.

'You're quite bossy,' he looked at her profile, holding it, watching as she pushed her hair behind her ear, her chiselled cheekbones an attractant.

She took her eyes briefly off the road to view him. 'Didn't my mother tell you?' She was only half joking. She still felt Natasha had a great deal to do with his asking her out.

'No. She just spoke about your beauty and intelligence... and so far, she hasn't been wrong.' He was smiling sweetly and she found herself laughing and warming to his obvious charm.

Parking as usual was near to impossible as they arrived, and they decided to chance it in the supermarket parking lot, Honey sweeping aside Kevin's concerns about the possibility of clamping after two hours.

'The most you'll get is a parking ticket,' she said flippantly and smiled cheekily.

'That's eased my mind,' he replied, mirroring her impudence.

Rolly-Polly was full to capacity, with a two-hour waiting list.

'What's so special about that place?' Kevin asked, slightly annoyed that they had driven all that way for nothing.

'It's been family run for decades, and I guess people really appreciate that touch. Sorry if you feel put out, I didn't realise it would be this full, although I know it's popular.'

Kevin took her hand as they walked back to the super-market parking lot, above them the overcast summer sky with the clouds completely still, a plane disappearing behind fluffy denseness.

'You don't ever need to apologise to me, Honey. I wasn't annoyed,' he said and Honey knew he had been annoyed even to make a reference.

'Can I ask you something personal?' Kevin now had her hand firmly clasped in his as they walked as naturally and normally as two young lovers.

'Depends what it is.'

'Are you free for me to love?'

Honey came to a halt, looking up at him. 'What a funny way to say something like that.'

'Are you? Because you do have this "unavailable" label tagged to you.'

She began walking again. 'It's far too soon for talk of love... did my mother put you up to this?'

It was Kevin's turn to halt abruptly. 'My interest in you, Honey, has nothing to do with your mother. So she goes on and on about you whenever I see her, but meeting you, being here with you now makes me know what I know.'

'And what do you know?'

'That I could easily love you... if you're free.'

'We haven't known each other long and you already know you could love me?'

'Yes. When you love someone, love doesn't wait for permission, love takes it.'

She held her breath as Kevin's words gave meaning to her internal battle against loving Ashley Elliott, a man she felt sure was so hurt by his ex, he wouldn't consider loving again anytime soon.

'That's not fair, I actually hate that thought. Love should wait for permission; it would be kinder to the heart.' She pouted.

'You sound like you're afraid of love.'

'Afraid? No. I'm only afraid of loving the wrong man.'

'That's not me,' he reached out and moved a strand of hair from her eye, just like Ashley would. 'Let's take some time getting to know each other, what do you say? We go at your speed.'

'Kevin, I'm all tied up on someone else. It's a bad idea to love me.'

'Is he tied up on you?'

She shook her head, bursting into a false laugh at the same time to avoid the knot of tears in her throat. 'I think so. But he's been hurt and isn't ready.'

'Then why are you wasting your time? Look how beautiful you are, so sexy and intelligent. He's an idiot if he can't see all you are. But I can. Give me a chance to show you what you'll be missing if you turn me down.'

'I'll crush you.'

'I'll take the chance. Look, no commitments, just take it a day at a time.'

She saw no harm in that, in fact it was the perfect way to eliminate Ashley Elliott from her mind.

As they pulled up in the cul-de-sac, Natasha gave an eager wave from the window and Kevin waved back.

'Thanks, Kevin—see you soon.'

'When?'

'Call me and I'll let you know.'

'Can I kiss you?' Before she could answer, his lips were on hers, gentle and tasting of peppermint. She was surprised to find she liked it.

Nineteen

July 2016

Honey felt light headed as she got out of bed that Friday morning for work, and she had to lie back down quickly. She closed her eyes wondering if she was getting the flu or some bug that thrived so happily in her stuffy office. She wouldn't think of taking the day off on a Friday, everyone knew that trick, so despite the weird light-headedness, she forced herself to shower and dress, taking her time until the feeling passed. The hours at work too passed quickly, and before she knew it, she was being driven by Kevin to Zeez's. She was disappointed when they arrived to find it was Fatty's day off and her and Fredrick had gone out for the day. Honey tried Fatty's phone and it rang out.

'We can still enjoy our dinner, even if your friend and her fiancé aren't here,' Kevin said, rather dejectedly after they had ordered. Honey immediately apologised for what she realised was inconsiderate behaviour.

'Oh, Kev, I'm sorry. It's just Fatty and Freddy are getting married and I haven't seen her in over a week—'

'And you haven't seen me in two,' he pointed out, with a fork in his hand.

Honey smiled. 'You have my undivided attention now.'

'That's all I've ever wanted,' Kevin leaned forward, pouting his lips in kiss mode. Honey hesitated, then kissed his mouth quickly.

'Can we do that again, only slower?' He thrust his head forward and she allowed him to take her lips with his, the unfamiliar feel surprisingly sensuous.

*

Fatty and Fredrick returned from their wedding shopping spree exhausted, and all they'd purchased were the white gold bracelets Fatty had chosen for the bridesmaids. Fredrick had loyally followed her from shop to shop as she decided she wanted something, only to change her mind. They'd already put a deposit on a three-bedroom house in Hendon, North West London which Fatty had fallen in love with.

'I never in a million years ever thought I could be so happy, Freddy,' Fatty snuggled close as they sat watching television. Fredrick's parents had gone to Brazil and they were alone in the house.

'You deserve so much happiness, Vanesse. I don't think I'll ever be able to repay you for the success of Zeez and how you've changed my life.' He hugged her, pulling her in close. 'It was hard watching you with that guy, the way he treated you was the talk of West London. I always dreamed of taking you away from that and making you my own and now I have.'

'I'm so glad I'm yours, Freddy, and it's all thanks to Hon. I wanted to sort out her love life and she ended up doing the same for me. I'll never be able to thank her enough.'

'Me neither,' Fredrick admitted. 'You know her mother was trying to match-make her and me?'

Fatty smiled knowingly. 'Yes, Hon did say.'

'We both knew how I felt about you and anyway, I'm so far from what Honey would want in a man, I'm nothing like Ashley Elliott.'

'Thank God!' Fatty laughed.

'Is Honey serious about him?'

'I'm not sure. I don't think so. But she's been sort of funny lately, not quite herself.'

'Well she has been seeing that Kevin. Maybe he's getting to her. You think?'

Fatty shrugged. 'God knows. Hon is so fussy and I don't think a few dinner dates will impress her with banker Kevin. I'll call and take her out on a spa day, she loves a spa.'

Fredrick placed a kiss on Fatty's forehead. 'You're a good friend, Honey's lucky.'

'Oh, Freddy, I'm the lucky one. Hon is the best.'

Fatty looked into the eyes of the man she loved so much she thought she would drown with the feeling. 'I love you and I can't wait to be your wife.'

❋

Honey was feeling lethargic, lying on her bed, fully aware that Fatty and Zhara would be arriving within the hour for their spa day. It was a good day for a spa, bright sun riddled July skies with a cool southerly wind. That funny feeling was plaguing her again. She felt sick, but not enough to throw up. It made her not want to eat, which had her feeling weak and faint, so it was great news when Fatty called to say their appointment at the spa had been shifted to afternoon, due to an oversight of the receptionist who had double booked. Fatty was fuming, but Honey was relieved. She snuggled back under her duvet, breathing in deep to still the nausea while her mind rummaged through what she ate, or kept eating that she may be allergic to. She made a mental note to make a doctor appointment if the feeling persisted. Her mobile rang and she placed it to her ear thinking it was Fatty with more spa updates.

'What did you forget to tell me this time?' Honey muffled into the phone.

'That I miss you... Hon-Hon.'

Her heart started skipping, the sick feeling in her stomach dispersing like smoke on a windy day. She half sat up, positioning the pillows to her comfort.

'Hi, Ashley,' she said hesitantly.

'How you been, girl?'

'Am good, you?'

'Yeah, bookings are coming in for Christmas already. What you doing now? Want to meet for a drink?'

'No, not a good idea.'

'Still hating on me? Still regretting our night of passion?'

Honey heaved to still the flutter that was her heart. 'Hardly remember it,' she lied, the flutter becoming erratic in her chest. She just wanted his voice out of her ear. How she missed hearing it. His silence confirmed his hurt and she was immediately sorry.

'Ashley, I think you and I wouldn't work—we got caught up in the pretend relationship, but this is real life and—'

'Are you trying to say you forget what we felt like together? Don't you remember kissing the breath out of me? Climbing on me like you were trying to get inside of me... you forget what we shared that night, really?'

'What do you want, Ashley? What the fuck do you want?'

'I miss what we had—'

'For fuck's sake! We didn't have anything, we were pretending, remember?'

'Some of it felt real... I guess I miss that part.'

Honey bit into her bottom lip, closing her eyes and clenching the phone to her ear. His voice kept that flutter in her chest going and she started seeing his lips, feeling his hands, *oh God am I going crazy?*

'Pass by the club later, there's a piano special going on and I know you love to listen to the piano.'

'Are you playing?' she asked.

She heard his laugh, not quite sure whether to call it cynical. 'No. A jazz singer by the name of Carmen el Noir. Come around 7:30pm, we can have a drink surrounded by people so you'll be safe.'

She allowed herself to laugh. 'I'm not afraid of you, Ashley Elliott, not in that sense.'

'Then in what sense are you afraid of me?'

'I'll let you know when I know.'

'If I were to go serious again, it would be with you, Hon-Hon.' She heard his breath and tried to interpret what it meant but couldn't even begin.

She wished she could believe him. 'I'll come to the club later. Fatty and Za are going to the spa with me this afternoon, so we might be later than 7:30.'

'Cool. See you later.'

✻

G West Spa was inconspicuously tucked away off the busy Uxbridge Road in Shepherds Bush. On approach, all you could see were the large, impenetrable wooden gates that opened automatically as you drove up to them. The huge glass and wooden building, magnificently put together with shapes varying from octagonal, diamond, squares, rectangles and circles, was exquisite in its awkwardness.

A short, uniformed figure made a little jog towards their car, his arms waving them to the left where Honey immediately saw the gate to the parking area.

'How long did you say we're booked for?' Zhara asked, grabbing her bag and taking out a pocket size mirror to view her face, beginning with her eyes.

'Za, don't tell me you've got makeup on to come to a

spa—'

'Of course she has, she's been seeing Ahmed, the fitness instructor in the gym,' Honey informed.

'And we pass the gym on the way to the sauna and steam rooms, so why not give myself a little help,' Zhara pouted, adding lip gloss.

'Crazy, stupid bitch,' Fatty got out of the car. 'He's divorced with two kids and living with his girlfriend.'

Zhara heaved. 'Yeah, I know, but he's been trying to leave her and he keeps texting me coz he wants me. I'm weak to him, I need you guys to strengthen me to avoid his delicious poison.'

'Stupid, crazy bitch,' Fatty repeated.

As they passed the gym, Ahmed came out and signalled to Zhara, his purple and black cycling shorts and matching vest top moulded as though they were painted on his muscular body. They left Zhara and headed down the hallway towards the women's changing rooms and spa, the cool and soothing pale apple coloured walls and the minty scented heat loosened their energy as they anticipated entering heaven. Honey had felt the same way when Ashley had pulled her towards him in his bed, as he started to undress her, kissing her passionately between every piece of clothing he peeled off. Why was she still thinking of him? Was it even a good idea to see him later? She still shook at the thought of him.

When Zhara joined them, they had already been in the steam room and sauna at twenty minutes intervals each time. They had relaxed, chatted and giggled away in the huge, bubbling Jacuzzi, mostly about Freddy and how wonderful he was.

'Sorry guys, Ahmed wanted to talk seriously to me.' Zhara joined them in the Jacuzzi, unable to keep that smile off her face. The one that tells the world that love or something close to it has touched this person's life.

'You're playing with fire, Za,' Fatty told her sternly. 'I mean, I can see the attraction—you really can't miss it when he's in them cycling shorts. Don't know how you can allow him to fool you though; he's living with his girlfriend and still married to his wife.'

Zhara shrugged her bony shoulders. 'He's getting a divorce, and that girl he lives with, he says he's not serious about, he just needs some place to live.'

'And you believe him,' Fatty scoffed.

'You guys fancy coming to the Club for drinks after this?'

'After this I'm meeting Freddy.'

'Not me,' Zhara said. 'I'm having Ahmed for dinner after his shift.'

'Must say Hon, I'm surprised you even want to go to the Club.' Fatty waded through the bubbling water closer to Honey.

'Ashley called and invited me,' she said super casually, thinking how just saying his name, or the sound of his name always flicked her heart.

'Thought you were seeing Kevin.' Fatty was up in her face now, a know-it-all look surrounding her.

'Kevin doesn't own me,' Honey said defensively. 'I'm just

feeling restless and want to do something different.'

'You'd tell me if there's anything I need to know about you and Ash, right?' Fatty had not moved from Honey's face.

'Me too, I want to know all the dirty,' Zhara laughed.

'You guys make me sick,' Honey moved away from Fatty, submerging herself in the bubbling pool and trying to make light of a moment that touched her truth.

'Come, we don't want to look like prunes,' Fatty was easing her way out of the water, her friends following her.

Honey was apprehensive about meeting Ashley on her own. She stood at one of the entrances of the circular bar and was instantly joined by Ashley, his smiling face genuine in its appreciation of seeing her.

'Glad you came, Hon-Hon. Come and have a drink, on the house. Have you eaten? Our chef is trying some new healthy stuff which I'm sure you'll like.' His hand rested gently on her waist as he guided her to sit at a table for two, tucked away at the back.

Honey nodded, acutely aware of his touch on her waist, the thought of his hand travelling her thighs suddenly flashed without her permission. 'I do feel hungry after the spa. I feel like I could eat a ton of chips, avocado and salted cucumber.'

'Chips and salad? Okay.' His smile was puzzled.

'And make sure the chips are fat and well done and crispy, no salt on them, just the cue.'

He laughed and signalled to a waiter who was by their table in two long strides, taking the order and flashing a friendly smile at Honey.

While they waited for the food, Honey sipping an elderberry juice and Ashley a Smirnoff, they chatted and laughed.

'It's nice seeing you again, Hon-Hon. You're looking good, glowing.'

Honey moved her mouth away from her glass to laugh. 'That will be the spa. Steam and sauna do great things for the skin.'

'So, what's going on with you? You still dating this Kevin?' Ashley asked with flippancy. Truthfully, the thought had been deranging his daily routine.

Honey thought this the opportunity to protect her heart. 'Yes, I'm seeing Kevin.'

There fell seconds of awkwardness, a mist of unbearable uncertainty for both. The waiter dispersed the mist, placing in front of Honey a plate of golden-brown fat chips, too tempting to restrain her hand from picking one up before the plate was lowered completely in front of her. Then followed a bowl of diced, square cucumber surrounded by sliced avocados.

'How's your love life?' she asked, blowing on the chip before taking a cautious bite and using a fork to spear a slice of avocado, which she swiftly devoured.

His arms were resting on the table, crossed. He wasn't hungry and was glad he hadn't ordered anything.

'I don't have one. I had a pretend one, but it ended.'

Honey stuffed more chips in her mouth accompanied by the cucumber and avocado. 'This tastes like heaven,' she closed her eyes in ecstasy. 'Seriously, it's delicious—taste some, you don't want to eat?' She pushed the near empty bowl of fried fat chips towards him.

'You want some more?' he asked. 'You must be hungry the way you tore into that.'

She nodded with an endearing guilty smile, which Ashley admitted was cute. 'I've been stuffing my face with this for the past month, it's like I'm craving it. Can I have another elderberry juice too? I'm addicted to that.'

With a wave of Ashley's hand, the waiter disappeared and returned with another bowl of the same, and Honey munched through them at the same speed.

'You want more?' Ashley asked in amused amazement. 'You can sure put food away. I didn't know you could eat so much,' he commented quickly, his eyes drinking her in, 'although is that a tummy I see poking through there?' He laughed at the horror on her face.

'You think I've put on weight? I've been thinking that too, on my waist?' She looked at the remaining chips with scorn but finished them anyway. 'That's it. No more fried potatoes for me.' She pulled the bowl of cucumber and avocado towards her and proceeded to finish it with the same relish.

'You don't want to try our baked chicken or fish? Drew is fresh off the boat from Jamaica, award winning chef I may add,' he boasted.

Honey thought about it. She had gone off chicken and her favourite fish dishes. She made a mental note to perhaps visit her doctor if this change of appetite didn't ease.

'Not feeling it, and honestly, I'm full,' she patted her stomach and was a little startled to feel that it really did feel round. She made a mental note to start exercising.

'So, if you're open to dating, can you and I date?'

'What about Bethany?'

Ashely was taken aback. 'What about her?'

'You tell me.'

'There's nothing to tell.'

He stood up and took one of her hands, pulling her to stand. 'Let's dance to this Mariah, I've always liked it.' His arms were around her waist, his closeness had the butterflies racing around her stomach and her body involuntarily melted into his slow-moving hips as Mariah Carey's *Always Be My Baby* filled the club.

He squeezed her in closer, the butterflies escaping to her heart. 'You're enjoying this, aren't you?' His lips felt soft against her ear.

'What am I enjoying?'

'My being totally crazy for you, and you not caring.'

Her eyes held him unwavering. 'We shouldn't have done what we did—'

'You honestly regret our night together?' She thought she saw pain flicker in his eyes fleetingly.

Confusion made her release the strength she had been accumulating to crush this thing she had for him. She walked back to the table, picking up her half empty elderberry juice, 'I'm going, thanks for the dinner. I'll see you around.' She left quickly before the smothering desire took control.

✱

The last week in July, Kevin surprised Honey with the offer of a weekend in Berlin to celebrate his thirty fifth birthday. She had never been before, and was still suffering from the ache in the heart that suspends appetite. She was getting depressed and feeling fat. She had started doing frantic sit-ups to flatten her stomach, and took up jogging despite her father laughing and telling her that the few inches gained suited her. She was not happy about her tummy, which she felt was sticking out a little more than before.

Her mother was over the moon when Honey told her she was going to Berlin for the weekend with Kevin. Natasha was relieved that her daughter was finally out of that strange relationship with Ashley Elliott, and secretly celebrated in her head, because Aaron had frowned when she mentioned how happy Honey would be with Kevin and that she hoped marriage was on the cards. She even secretly started surfing the web for marriage sites and wedding planners.

Honey was feeling apprehensive about her Berlin trip, but was determined to go. When she had agreed, Kevin was so happy, his smile lighting up his face and softening his eyes. He had looked grateful and she had felt guilty, newly determined to love him in any way she could.

Her first impression as the taxi drove them to their hotel in Berlin was how clean the streets were for a capital city.

'You okay?' Kevin smiled at her, his eyes cautious.

She nodded, looking out of the car window, taking in the Burger King, Santander Bank, TK Maxx and thinking how everywhere in the world was somehow interconnected and the rich owned everything. She even gave a giggle as they passed a Woolworth store; her father had pictures with his own mother outside a Woolworth store as a child in the 1970s. Within forty-five minutes, the taxi was pulling up onto a narrow-cobbled street made up of small, even, stone slabs, and at the end of the street, an impressive building with the sign: Welcome to Hotel Berlin, in bold orange, italic letters. The receptionist, a tall, athletic blond, whose hair was pulled tightly back into a bun, and whose eyes smiled sweetly at them as they walked in, offered them a drink, which they refused. After signing in they were shown to their room, a double 'T' shape room with the shower immediately on the left as you entered, a large mirror stuck to the front of the teak built in wardrobe and facing the shower door. Once past the threshold, the king size bed made the apprehension return.

As if sensing her hesitation, Kevin placed the hand luggage down by the wardrobe and took hold of her hand. 'You sure you're okay?'

She looked at him and felt panicked but hoped he didn't sense it. Without a second thought, she wrapped her arm around his neck and kissed him before she could change her mind and run for the door, onto the plane, and back home in her comfort zone. She felt his response, urgent but gentle, his lips hungry as he sucked her lips. It was different from Ashley's kiss and with that thought she started stripping. She thought once Kevin made love to her, Ashley would disappear from her mind, and would take the memory of his hands from her body. Kevin was a tentative lover, so willing to explore and please her. She was surprised that her body reacted and responded to him, that when he entered her, she was ready, willing, and desperate for someone to erase and replace Ashley Elliott.

After taking a shower together, Honey felt relaxed and could easily believe her life was about to change. They walked hand in hand in search of the restaurant the receptionist recommended, passing a canal, its water muddy, murky, and still.

'This is my favourite city,' Kevin said as they entered the restaurant, which in all honesty looked like a converted old barn from the outside.

'Why?' Honey frowned. She was not impressed with what she had so far seen, other than the clean streets.

Kevin laughed and hugged her to him. Inside the barn was a pleasant surprise for Honey. The custard coloured papier mache stone walls added a unique, antiquated look, and with men and women made out of straw stuck to the walls like pictures, Honey felt she was having a cultural experience. She couldn't wait to tell Fatty and Zhara. Sitting on the solid pine coloured bench, facing Honey, Kevin ordered salted roast of pork neck with red cabbage and potato dumplings. Honey settled for salted herring fillet with fried potatoes.

'You are beautiful, Honey. I think I'm falling in love with you.'

She looked startled, not sure what to say, the uneasy filling her again. She laughed, nervously. 'Kev, let's take things slow.'

'As slow as you like,' he reached out to move her hair from

her eyes, like Ashley would do, and she was once again left thinking about Ashley. 'I don't want to do anything that might make you feel bad. I want you to be happy, Honey. Let's take the U and try and find our way to the Berlin Wall.'

'What's the U?'

'The underground.'

Honey frowned. 'Really? You have the energy for all that? I'm tired,' she said as she tried to hold down a yawn.

'Okay, tomorrow we get up at the crack of dawn and find our way there,' Kevin enthused. 'We can't come to Berlin and not see the Wall.'

Kevin was an early bird. Honey was not. Hadn't been for the past few months, if she were to be honest. It would take her a while before the nauseous feeling, which came and went of its own will, subsided. So, when Kevin was up, showered, and making as much noise as possible to get her up, she grabbed the pillow and put it over her head.

'I've got some tea here for you,' he tried coaxing her, failing badly. 'Okay. Shall we just walk the streets and find a restaurant? Get us some breakfast and some real tasting coffee.'

Honey moved the pillow and squinted up at him. 'Can't you keep still for once? Must you always be on the go?'

'Let's stay in bed all day,' Kevin suggested. 'Let's just watch our favourite movies with subtitles. Drink beer, make love, more German subtitled movies, make more love and...'

'Okay, give me an hour to shower and dress.'

Kevin laughed. 'I'll go and get some directions from the receptionist and meet you downstairs. I want to impress you,

Honey. Please let me.'

She smiled at him. 'Just stop trying so hard.'

*

Back in London late Sunday night, Kevin had the taxi drop Honey home before kissing her passionately and telling her he would call her in the morning. Natasha was waiting up as she opened the front door and was there taking Honey's hand luggage while peeling her coat off.

'Was it fun?' she asked her daughter, not stopping for a response. 'Of course it was, Kevin is a great entertainer. How was Berlin?'

Honey suddenly felt exhausted, and talking was the last thing she wanted to do or listen to.

'Didn't get time to see much of the city. Saw lots of ten-month pregnant men. Yuk!'

Natasha squeezed her shoulder. 'You're too British. But at least you had good company.'

'Yes,' Honey nodded. 'Kev is very sweet,' she said, noting her mother's I told you so smile.

After she showered, Honey called Fatty to tell her she was back.

'That was quick—it's like you went yesterday,' Fatty beamed.

'Well that's how weekends go, quick like the wind.'

'Was it good? Did you have fun? What's Kev boy like as a lover?'

Honey yawned, snuggling under her duvet. 'If I wasn't so tired, I'd laugh.'

'So, he's that bad? Did you even come?'

'Fats! Quit.'

'That bad, huh?'

'No,' Honey snapped. 'He's very caring.'

'My God! You don't want caring when you're having sex! You want passion, you want it rough, you want it good and hard but you do not want it fucking caring. Shit! Well it won't last, this relationship you have going—not if his sex is caring, for fuck sake.'

'Goodnight, Fats,' Honey cut off the phone as Fatty's laughter exploded in her ear.

Monday morning was not welcome. Honey turned over in her bed to still her phone alarm on the bedside table. 6:45am. The feeling was back, that sea-sick nauseous feeling in her stomach and a strange taste of metal in her mouth. She closed her eyes, knowing sleep was the only way through this.

Her mother's voice brought her out of her stupor. She bolted upright, shocked by the strong streak of light her mother let into the bedroom as she pulled the drapes apart.

'You're still in bed,' Natasha said accusingly. 'It's after mid-day. You didn't go to work?'

Honey flopped back on the bed, a hand on her forehead. 'Obviously,' she groaned, pulling the duvet over her head.

'Did you call in sick to work? Let them know you weren't coming in? Oh, Honey,' Natasha heaved because she knew by the twist of her daughter's body under the duvet, that she hadn't. 'Jobs are not so easy to come by. I'll go and call your manager and tell her some little white lie. You need to get up and sort your head out. Did Kevin tire you out so much?' Natasha smiled, happy in the thought that things were serious between them.

Thirty minutes later Honey went downstairs, showered, dressed and feeling a whole lot better, hoping her mother had gone back to work. No such luck. Tasha was perched on the bar stool sipping her coffee as Honey entered the kitchen.

'I called Kevin and told him you're home. He didn't go to work either and says he's been calling you. He's on his way to take you to lunch. I told him you'd over slept and hadn't eaten.'

Honey sighed. 'Tasha, you need to stop minding my business. And why aren't you at work?'

'Well, I'm going now. I just popped home because I forgot my glasses and of course I had to call your very understanding manager and explain your absence. By the way, you've got a bout of food poisoning from Berlin.' Tasha made her way to the door and hesitated. 'You should make a bit of an effort to fix up a little,' she waved a hand over Honey's navy-blue sweat suit, pointing to her hair. 'Fix up like when you were dating that Ashley boy, Kevin is worth it.'

Tasha left and Honey sat watching the door for a long moment before she allowed herself to move, to think. Why did Tasha have to inject him into her thoughts now? Stir up all that stuff she had been working so hard to delete, his lips giving way to that seductive smile whenever he looked at her, his eyes closing when he laughed. The way he held her, made love to her with confidence, passion and tenderness. Honey shrugged her shoulders and headed upstairs. She flung open her wardrobe door and pulled out a fitted Karen Millen dress, silk and patterned with light blue roses. She climbed into the dress and found the side zip wouldn't budge. She had gained inches but there was no time to think about it, Kevin would be arriving soon thanks to Tasha. It wasn't that she wasn't looking forward to seeing him, but no, she wasn't looking forward to seeing him. She had seen him yesterday, spent the whole weekend with him. She could honestly do with a break, which made her feel guilty. She pulled out her pastel pink jersey dress. It was short sleeved and would look good with her knee length boots. She brushed her hair back into a ponytail because there really was no time to attempt anything else. As she sprayed some Gucci perfume over her dress the doorbell rang. Kevin.

Her smile, though painted on, was totally relaxed as she allowed Kevin to gather her into his arms. She couldn't quite face his kiss and buried her face in his chest.

'You smell divine, Honey, good enough to eat,' his nibbles started on her cheek and carried on to the nape of her neck. 'Is anyone home?' he asked suggestively.

Honey withdrew from his arms abruptly, a frown across her forehead. She didn't want to make love with Kevin in her bed. She didn't want those memories. 'Let's get going for lunch. We can go to Zeez.'

Kevin heaved. Honey had noticed that he liked to heave a lot. 'We mostly eat there—'

'I enjoy the food, Kev, and yes, I get to see my bestie. You want me relaxed, right?'

Kevin smiled. 'Come on you,' he pulled her lightly and placed a soft kiss on her lips, 'I want you any which way.'

Zeez was packed at lunch time, but Fatty made space for Honey and Kevin by placing a table for two at the front of the restaurant under the awnings. It was pleasantly mild for this last day of July and Honey ordered off the menu, her usual. Chunky fried chips, avocado and cucumber salad, adding jerk chicken.

Fatty laughed as she placed the plate before Honey. 'I don't know why you've developed this craving for the same thing instead of our delicious cuisine, but enjoy anyway.' She placed a plate of jerk pork and sweet potato chips in front of Kevin. 'Enjoy.' She smiled before leaving them.

Kevin poured himself a glass of wine. Honey covered her glass as he attempted to fill hers.

'Not for me, I'll have sparkling water. I've noticed it helps my digestion.'

'Did you enjoy Berlin?' Kevin asked before a fork filled with pork and sweet potato chips disappeared into his chewing mouth. It was a heaped fork, Honey noticed, wondering why it amused her, and she decided she really did like him and all his quirkiness.

'We didn't see much of it,' she pointed out, using her fingers to pull a strip of meat from the jerked chicken.

'Want to go again next weekend?'

She shook her head. 'Berlin? Again? No.'

'Why? You didn't enjoy it?'

'Like I said, I didn't see much of it.'

He cut through some more of the meat on his plate and chewed thoughtfully, watching her, the activity of thoughts clear on his face.

'Do you like spending time with me?' He asked, still chewing.

She nodded, nibbling a chunky chip. 'Of course, it should be obvious.'

He peered at her over the wine glass he took a sip from. 'But it's not. I'm not sure how you really feel about me. You have a funny way of looking at me sometimes, and I don't know what the look means, but it means something.'

Honey was unperturbed. 'Well, when you can tell me what look you're talking about I'll be able to tell you what it means.'

'The next time you give it to me, I'll point it out.'

She laughed.

'At least I can make you laugh...' She liked him, she decided. She really liked him. And just as she had accepted the idea, she heard that familiar voice.

'Hi Honey.' Ashley rarely called her Honey, and for some reason it felt like a sharp sting, as if he had used a large elastic band to ping her in the middle of her stomach. His eyes were coloured with unfamiliar feelings. The amber pools were frosty.

'Hi,' she finally said, 'how are you?'

Ashley laughed, or maybe it was meant to be a laugh but a cough got tangled with it along the way, making it unclear as to what she had actually heard. Kevin was looking at her with a question mark.

'Ashley, this is Kevin. Kevin, this is Ashley.'

Kevin forced a smile and a nod of his head. Ashley didn't.

'Do your thing,' he told her, walking off, but not before she recognised the blatant accusation pooling in his eyes.

'Who's that to you?' Kevin asked.

'The truth? Nothing.' She was astounded at how it hurt her to say that. But she convinced herself if she said it enough, it would become the truth one day.

Twenty

Ashley was lying on the leather sofa in the Studio staring at the ceiling; the only thought in his head was Honey and her lunch date with that Kevin dude. She looked happy too. He winced just thinking about it, about her with him. He had an afternoon meeting with Marla to sign off on the new property, but after coming across Honey, that pink dress looking so hot on her, all he wanted to do was drag her away from that man. How could she, was the all absorbing question in his head. Did their night together mean so little to her? He reached for his glass of JD on the coffee table and took a swig before lying back down. Yet thinking back to that night it was she who initiated everything, she who pulled off his clothes, her passion hungry, tender, pursuing and focused on extracting the pleasures she wanted. Her lips, her eyes, they had been swathed with feelings and emotions deeper than he'd ever seen and it was delicious.

'Ash, this is the third time I'm asking, I'm going to grab some fish and chips, you want some?'

Standing at the partially opened door was Dame, kitted

out in stone wash denim, Doc Marten boots and his flagship pink tee shirt.

'Pick up a bottle of JD.'

'There's still a quart in the bottle—'

'Buy another.'

Dame frowned, stepped inside and closed the door. He sat on the single sofa, his eyes pooling with questions as he stared at Ashley.

'You wouldn't keep anything from me, would you? Everything okay with business?' Dame asked.

Ashley tore his eyes from the ceiling and met Dame's. 'Yes. Never been better.'

Dame gave a small sigh of relief. 'Then what the fuck is up with you and this depressing shit?'

'You gonna get the JD or what?' Ashley snapped.

'Is it Honey Fontaine?'

Ashley sat upright, staring fiercely at Dame.

'Ah ha, I see. Wow! Not sure what to say. You feeling her that bad? Are you scared to try again?'

'What the fuck are you asking, Dame? No! I want to try again. Bethany is history.'

'You got the Honey bug, Ash. It's the only explanation for your behaviour since meeting her. You want her, don't you? Really want her.'

'Yes. I do. But I don't want no woman who don't want me!'

'So, you want her but she don't want you. Ouch. Yes, that'll hurt, but have you told her how you feel?'

'Dame, are you for real!'

'Are you?' Dame became serious. 'You and Honey began playing some crap game to fool her Moms, but she got under your skin during that time. I see it with my own pretty blue eyes. Not even Beth had you this way.'

Ashley entwined his fingers, pressing his thumbs together in frustration. He loosened his hands and leaned back. 'You're right, I like her more than any other girl. She's a challenge I can tell you.' He broke off to laugh. 'She has this way of sweeping me with her eyes, of disapproving every fucking move I make, every word I say, it gets me.' He sighed. 'Now she's fulfilling her mother's wish and hanging out with some rich jock... I can't do anything about that. A girl wants what a girl wants.'

'You can maybe tell her how you feel.'

'Tried. She doesn't take me seriously, she's not interested.'

*

Marla unzipped her jacket, letting out her generous breasts, which seemed as though they were being reluctantly restrained behind her white lace blouse. She sat facing Ashely in the studio office, and leaned forward to pick up his glass of JD, emptying it with one swallow.

'I needed that,' she said, stretching out her bare legs in front of her. 'We had a meeting this afternoon. I waited, I called and no response from you. You could've called to cancel, Ash.'

'Sorry, girl. My head's full of other stuff.'

Love Again

'What stuff? The books are healthy, your accounts are fat and things are looking good. The small hotel in Manchester was the perfect investment and the house you bought for your moms, all rented until she's ready to move in.'

'Right now Moms has been playing up again, so I've got to go over there tomorrow.'

'She stopped taking her meds again?'

He nodded, feeling tearful at the thought of his mother. Marla squeezed his hand.

'You're so good to your Moms, Ash. I really admire the way you care for her and your little sis. How is Marley?'

'She's good. Going to study Fashion and Design at college in September. I worry about her though, the way she hates on our Moms. It has no let-up. But then, Moms ignore her all the time. Acts as if she doesn't exist, thanks to my so-called father.'

'Poor woman. Do you think she'll ever get better?'

Ashley contemplated this as though it wasn't something he did all the time. 'I hope so. I really hope so, but I honestly don't know.'

'You need a break, you work too hard. Take a week or two—go visit Nathan,' Marla suggested.

'Not the time for that.'

'You know Bethany has been calling me. She wants you to forgive her—'

Ashley heaved. 'There's no coming back for Beth and me—she did what she did and I'm over it. I don't want any messages from her, and she knows it.'

Ashley poured himself another drink.

'You know Ash, ever since Honey, there are times when you change into someone I don't recognise.'

∗

The first weeks of August had been a blur for Honey as her workload increased and Kevin became a regular feature of her world. She blamed him for the inches she was putting on, his swanning her off to expensive Mayfair and West End restaurants, which he rightly pointed out that she rarely finished any of the foods ordered, so it was not this making her gain weight. In the end she did what she always said she wouldn't. She joined a gym. Only she couldn't get the time to attend regularly enough and ended up buying some Fitness DVDs, which she hardly viewed because she was always so tired.

'Can you stop stressing over your weight? You have no weight,' Fatty told Honey as they drove down the Uxbridge road towards Shepherd's Bush to do some market shopping. 'If there's anyone with a weight problem, it's me, and I ain't stressing over my size, not when Freddy loves it so much.' She sniggered.

'I'm not really stressing,' Honey spoke thoughtfully, 'it's just weird how my jeans are feeling tight.'

'And you're surprised after eating them chunky chips every chance you get?'

Honey gave into a smile. 'I do have a thing for them, but I'll stop.'

'You skinny girls get on my nerves. You're like a stick and

still think you're fat.'

'No, not fat, but my jeans are feeling tighter.'

'Thanks to the chunky chips,' Fatty wagged a finger.

They parked on one of the side roads, ensuring they paid for a parking ticket before walking off towards the market. Shepherds Bush Market was once very famous and when Honey was younger, she always looked forward to Saturday shopping with her mother. Honey, through her young eyes, saw it as a carnival. She remembered large crowds and the long black chauffeur driven limousines parked illegally by the side of the road, to let what seemed like a dozen black capes come out. Of course, those capes were women, Muslim women in their modest attires. What she remembered most about those women was the way they smelt. Their perfume, alluring, smooth, rich—they had intrigued her.

Her mother seemed to know everyone, as she went from stall to stall, if not to buy, then to have a little chat, even if it was about the weather or an update on someone's ill-health. Honey remembered the reggae music that floated out of the record shop, and how that shop was always full to the brim with mostly boys and young men, dancing, singing along to the music, big laughter and loud voices, marijuana mingling with cigarettes. No one seemed to care.

Now Shepherds Bush Market had changed, and the bustling and variety of stalls, although reduced, had been replaced by new shops and stalls, mainly selling food and goods aimed at Muslim, Polish, African and Caribbean communities. Apart from the traditional name brand supermarkets, the shop fronts donned mannequin draped in Hijabs and colourful scarfs, as the smell of falafel, chips and grilled meats saturated the air along the pavements. The aromatic burning incense mixed with Shisha smoke had become the traditional scent of Shepherds Bush. However, Natasha still had her favourite fishmonger based in the market, and so at least once a month Honey would have to go and collect the box of fresh fish, which were all scaled and washed, ready for collection.

'Let's pop in and see Za, haven't heard from her all week and when that happens it's usually because that fool she's giving her heart to has her not knowing her Fridays from her Mondays,' Fatty suggested, leading Honey by the hand. 'Oh look,' she pointed, dragging Honey in the direction of a gathering crowd. 'Let's see what's going on.'

Their pace slowed as they neared the renovated shop front. It was the opening of a new hair salon, its name boldly running along the awnings, reading *'Leyla's Salon.'*

'I wonder where the bitch got the cash from to open something like this,' Fatty spat, looking at Honey for agreement. 'I bet she got it all from lying on her back.'

'Fats, you're something else you are. Maybe the girl won the lotto or something, or maybe her grandma left her some money.'

'No, she used to work the same estates as Bella up to last year, or at least the year before.'

'Well, maybe she was saving up for all those years—'

'Or she got herself a sugar daddy more like it. Let's go inside—'

'I thought we were going to see Za... don't go making any trouble, Fats.'

'Yes, Mummy Honey.' Fatty smiled innocently before making a path through the small gathering and entering the shop. It was near impossible to get any further and Fatty turned to tell Honey to turn around, only Honey wasn't to be seen. Making her way out of the shop, Fatty saw Honey being held by her arms, a teenage boy on either side of her. Rushing towards them, Fatty was intercepted by a young woman holding up a hand and flapping it frantically.

'She passed out, the boys managed to grab her before she hit the ground.'

Fatty looked dazed. She took Honey's arm away from one of the boys. 'What you doing passing out, girl? You were right behind me, what happened? Did you trip?'

The fuzz was wearing off and Honey took some deep breaths. 'No. At least I don't think so. I felt... I don't even know,' she shook her head in confusion.

'Never mind. Let's get back to the car, I'll drive,' Fatty supported her with an arm around her waist, taking slow steps.

'Fats, I'm not that sick that we have to walk like two old ladies, I'm just a little dizzy.'

'Why?'

'Huh?'

'There must be a reason for your dizziness. Maybe you're anaemic? We bleed every month so it's not surprising—go to the health shop and get some iron tonic or something.'

Honey fell into silence. Her period hadn't been that

regular, ever since she got the contraceptive implant. She thought maybe it might have something to do with her feeling unwell for the past few months although she couldn't think why, when the implant had been in her arm for over a year.

The first thing Honey did Monday morning was phone the GP to make an appointment before work. She was lucky, the GP had a slot and she made her way out of the house to get to the 07:45am appointment on time.

Her GP was in the Fitz-Herbert Medical Centre, less than twenty minutes from her work, so her only anxiety was wrapped up in the queasy feeling in the pit of her stomach.

Dr Sterling appeared at the entrance of the waiting room and called her name. He smiled quickly and she followed him into his small surgery, his desk taking up most of the room, followed by the intimidating examining table. She sat down, her eyes scanning the four walls, which were bare, barring a picture of five children surrounding a beautiful brunette woman.

'It's been a while since I've seen you, Honey. How can I assist?'

Honey began feeling silly. She wasn't exactly sick, she knew that, and now she was feeling like she was wasting the doctor's time.

'It's probably nothing and I feel so silly taking up your time—'

'What exactly worries you?' His kind eyes put her at ease.

'I don't know. I feel sick a lot. First it was in the mornings and I couldn't get out of bed, I was that tired. Then the sick feeling would come and go but I've been feeling alright until last Saturday when I felt dizzy and sort of passed out. I think I may be anaemic,' she announced expressively.

Dr Sterling smiled. 'How long have you been feeling this way?'

She shrugged because she suddenly couldn't remember feeling free of this queasiness for a while.

'More than two months?' The doctor asked, tapping his keyboard and bringing his screen to life.

Honey considered hard. 'Yes, definitely.'

He asked her to pull up her sleeve and took her blood pressure.

'That's all normal,' he responded to her worrying look. 'Do you think you could be pregnant?' he asked.

Honey nearly jumped out of her seat. She stared at him in disbelief but couldn't answer for what seems like years.

'No—no, I couldn't be. I have the implant in, I can't be.'

The Doctor stood up. 'Can you hop up on the table? Let me have a feel of your tummy,' he told her.

She did as she was told, wondering why she should go along with this, feeling her stomach wasn't going to prove anything other than she had put on weight. It kept going through her head as Dr Sterling's firm hands prodded her abdomen.

'Let's get a urine test done,' he told her, opening the drawer and handing her a plastic tube. 'If you can, try and do a sample, please,' he smiled softly.

Honey's hand was shaking as she handed the doctor the

tube with her pale-yellow urine. He went over to a cupboard, his back turned so she could not see what he was doing. When he turned around, the small strip of paper in his hand, he asked her to sit down.

'Honey, you're pregnant.'

She looked startled. 'I can't be. I've got my implant—'

'No contraceptive is one hundred percent, Honey. You are definitely pregnant.'

Panic gripped her. She wasn't ready for a baby. She hadn't planned on having children for years to come. This was a nightmare. She sensed Kevin would want marriage as soon as she told him. She could see her mother's face, proud and happy that Kevin turned out to be the one. She really liked him but wasn't sure she wanted to spend the rest of her life with him.

'I'd like to arrange an abortion,' she told him calmly.

The Doctor looked at her softly. 'You need time to think things through. It certainly isn't too late to have an abortion; my estimation is that you're about fifteen weeks—'

A new fear stirred in Honey. 'Sorry, what did you say? Fifteen weeks? Impossible.'

'A rough guess, give a week or so, but I'm sure—'

'I should be five or six weeks, not fifteen—' she trailed, unable to finish her sentence, the truth pushing its way forward in the most flamboyant way, whistling, shouting, laughing. The truth is, if she was fifteen weeks pregnant, then the baby she was carrying belonged to Ashley Elliott.

Twenty-One

September 2016

Honey ran away. She felt really silly for it, but she ran away. She didn't go to work. Instead, she returned home, packed a weekend bag, jumped in her car and hit the A1. She drove for an hour and a half before she turned off and registered a sign. The sign said Welcome to Arlesey, so she drove into what seemed like a sleepy little village, pulling into the first B&B she saw off the narrow road. She used her credit card to make the payment then settled under the strange smelling duvet and cried. How had this happened? She was pregnant. Having Ashley Elliott's baby. All those sit-ups to flatten her stomach, the body work out videos, the diet she put herself on after eating her favourite chunky chips, was the baby even going to be normal?

She woke up to darkness in the room and suddenly felt afraid. She reached out and switched on the bedside lamp. It was only 10pm. She picked up her phone and immediately texted her mother, telling her she was fed up and wanted a few days to herself and included Fatty and Zhara. Then she turned her phone off.

*

Ashley was sat at the desk, absorbed in front of his computer, his mother's face smiling from the screen saver. He was looking over family pictures and didn't look up when Bethany entered the room. Suddenly sweat burst along her forehead and her hands became moist and heated.

Ashley turned to the sound from the door, a frown splitting his face as he saw Bethany. He looked at his watch, 4:15pm. Honey would be leaving work in forty-five minutes; she still filled his thoughts.

'Hi Ash,' Bethany walked slowly, stopping a few yards away as his glare halted her.

He returned his focus to the computer screen. 'Why are you here?' he asked without looking at her.

'Oh, I thought, I was in the area,' she played nervously with her fingers. 'I wanted to see you, to talk—'

'Why? There's nothing for you and I to talk about,' he told her moodily, his attention still on the screen.

Bethany swallowed her nervousness. 'I'm sorry, Ash. I'm so sorry I hurt you. Bruce was nothing. I was feeling lonely, you know, you worked long hours and I felt neglected—'

He stood up and reached for the paper from the printer, scrutinising the contents. 'I don't want to hear it. That's history.'

He dragged his eyes away from the paper to look at

Bethany. She was out of place here. He got used to not seeing her. The only girl he ever tried loving slept with a business partner and the betrayal was unforgivable, in his eyes. 'I still work long hours, even longer now, so you'd still be lonely, even if I gave it another chance.' He viewed her with indifference.

'Ash, I'm so sorry. I'll do anything to make it up, anything,' Bethany announced with a confidence they both knew was fake.

'You need to go.' He sat back down, placing the paper on the desk.

'Bruce used me, he just wanted to get back at you because you're financially better off than him. He only ever wanted to talk about you and what you'd do next—' she trailed feebly as his head turned slowly and he turned to stone.

'The way I'm built, Beth, I would never trust you again, and any woman I'm giving my time to, I would have to trust. You're not that woman.'

Bethany was choked by her tears and couldn't speak clear. 'Ash... please... please,' a sob caught in her. 'Please, I love you so much, Ash—if I could just—'

Ashley stood up, agitated. 'I let you into my life, Beth. I opened up to you, I thought we had something good. But you showed me otherwise. Bruce Joseph? You took your clothes off for that man? A man who only wanted to use you to get back at me. You know, you made me think I would never love again. There's no going back.'

She started crying. 'Please, please give me a chance. Don't be like this, Ash. Everyone deserves a second chance.'

'You need to go.' He told her as he started putting on his jacket.

She held onto his arm. 'Oh God, Ash, please, don't do this.'

'Do what?' He shook her off. 'Beth! Everything you asked me for, you got. I gave you it all—'

'Except your time! You didn't have any time for me! What was I supposed to do? I was lonely. Material things can't hold me, hug me, talk to me—'

'I'm in a hurry.' He cut her short, her words echoing, causing some discomfort.

Bethany felt she was fighting for her life. Ashley wouldn't trust her again. 'So, what will I do?' she pleaded. 'I need you, Ash. Please.'

He was walking out the door, Bethany hurrying behind him. Ashley stopped only to talk to Dame. 'I'm going to my next appointment. If Orlando comes, tell him I'll be back in an hour.'

Once outside, Ashley proceeded to place his briefcase on the passenger seat. A hurling brick crushed Bethany's lungs and heart together, as she watched him get into his car and drive off, taking her reason for existing with him. The pain was indescribable. She had hoped he could have remembered their good times together and forgive her. Now her sinking heart confirmed what her brain knew from the outset: Ashley Elliott would never forgive her. Yet she loved him. She loved him until the very thought of not having him in her life was unthinkable. His car disappeared among the traffic. He would

never allow her near him again, this much she knew, and it
sent her world crashing.

Twenty-Two

Honey drove back into London after spending two days in the B & B in Arlesey, no closer to knowing what to do about being pregnant. She hadn't called her manager, and only now did she start feeling panicky about it. It was very possible that she didn't have a job and she'd never needed one more. Parking off Kensington High Road, she walked slowly, her mind in chaos. The nauseous feeling was back, only now she had a name for it. Morning sickness, even if it came at differing times of the day. Honey stood anxiously inside the entrance of Zeez's, waiting for Fatty, her head swimming with the news she had to tell her. Finally, Fatty came out of her office and beckoned Honey to come. They sat on the small two seat sofa, two cups of cappuccino on the coffee table before them, accompanied by two fat blueberry muffins. The office was airy and bright and there was no doubt that Fatty had improved the place. Honey impulsively threw her arms around Fatty's neck.

'Forgive me?'

Fatty hugged her. 'For what?'

'For going off for three days without contact.'

'We're on the phone most days, we text, if you want time

out—'

'Yes, but I don't want us to lose seeing each other, I miss you.'

'You mushy cow,' Fatty laughed, 'you okay? Everything okay with Kevin?'

Honey sighed heavily and shrugged.

Fatty looked quizzical. 'What's the real reason you went off behind God's back to Arlesey? Where on earth is that?'

'Bedfordshire. I just drove and ended up there. I got scared,' Honey lowered her voice to a whisper.

'Of who? Let me have their name and I'll kick the shit out of them.'

'Not anyone, I got scared of a situation.'

Fatty looked more puzzled. 'Is that Kevin one of them sneaky good for nothing strips of shit? Undercover abuser? What did he do? I'll rip the motherfucker to pieces.'

Honey sighed and Fatty suddenly changed the topic, unable to contain the excitement she felt.

'Okay, I can sometimes be OTT but enough about you and your missing days! Freddy is going to Dubai next week and he wants me to go with him, just for ten days. Did you know they've opened a branch of Zeez out there?'

'That's great news, Fats. Are you sure you'll be alright with flying? You're scared stiff of heights.'

Fatty's eyes clouded. 'I can do anything with Freddy beside me,' she passed a cup of coffee to Honey.

Honey shook her head frantically, making a face. Her hand flew to her mouth and she stood up and rushed to the toilet. When she came back five minutes later, Fatty was open-mouthed.

'Can you move those cups of coffee please?' Honey held a tissue to her mouth as she sat down.

Fatty quickly moved the coffees to the other side of the room, and cracked the window. She turned and walked towards Honey, stopping a few inches away. Her hands went out to touch Honey's stomach.

'Are you pregnant?' Her eyes were wide and incredulous.

Honey flopped down on the sofa. She was actually dreading telling Fatty. Fatty had been trying to have a baby with Freddy and nothing had happened so far. Now she felt guilty. If only she could trade with Fatty—give her the use of her womb, she was sure one day soon technology would develop enough to make such an operation possible.

'Yes.' Honey sounded miserable.

Fatty looked at her friend in wonder. Honey was going to be a mum. Tears sprang to Fatty's eyes. She was happy and sad all in one. Honey was two years younger and would be a mother before her. Fatty knew the reason for her not getting pregnant, despite trying, was her childhood trauma. The doctors couldn't find anything and just said she should stop worrying and relax. Freddy agreed with them.

'You don't look pregnant, are you sure?' Fatty was looking in amazement at Honey. She sat close to her. 'What's it feel like?' Her smile was soft, her eyes glazed and dreamy.

Honey shrugged. She was more concerned about what she was going to say to her mother, Kevin and, more importantly,

Ashley.

'I just feel sick when I smell certain foods and drinks, like that coffee. I piss a lot more and, oh yeah, my breasts tingle, only I didn't know what the signs were.'

'Oh Hon, you're so lucky,' Fatty hugged her. 'Though I didn't think you and Kevin had it going like that. I thought you were just dating and having fun. You got caught, right?'

Honey stared glumly, her eyes suddenly filling with tears. 'Oh, Hon, don't cry,' Fatty gave her a comforting hug. 'I'll help you look after the rugrat and I know Za will too, if she can get from under Ahmed. Have you told Kevin?'

Honey shook her head.

'Do you think he'll be mad with you?'

Honey burst into tears, her arms going around her friend's neck as she hugged her tightly, all the time crying at her conflicted feelings.

'Listen, if he gets mad when you tell him, I want to know about it. I only like him because you do, understand. The minute you hate him, I hate him too. I'll come with you to tell him.' Fatty was patting her friend's back.

Honey finally managed to stop crying.

'Oh Fats, it won't be. It can't. Nothing will ever be okay again. It's not Kevin's, it's Ashley's baby.'

Fatty looked staggered. She held Honey at arm's length before releasing her. 'Ash? When? I mean, have you still been seeing him?'

'No,' Honey shook her head miserably. 'It happened only once. Once, I swear. Well, three times in one night, but only one occasion. I can't believe this. When the doctor told me I was pregnant I thought it was Kev's. But when he said I was fifteen weeks pregnant, I knew it was Ashley's—'

'I didn't even know that you and Ash... you acted like you were in total control... fuck sake! Oh fuck, fuck, fuck! What you going to do?'

'I'll tell Ashley last. First thing is to tell Kev, then I have to break the news to Tasha. She'll be totally pissed.'

'That's putting it lightly. She's going to kill your cute arse. You won't live to see your next birthday. Are you going to keep the baby?'

When she had thought it was Kevin's child, she was planning on an abortion. The baby being Ashley's, the secret ruler of her heart, had put a different tint on things. She was scared for the future but she didn't want to abort his baby.

'I think so. With Ashley and Tasha to tell, God knows I'm sick with worry. They'll both want to kill me. Oh, Fats, what a fucking mess.'

✽

Not only was she pregnant, but she had been given her notice for taking the three days off work without contacting her manager or answering their calls. It was the worst time really, because she needed a job more than ever now, but somehow she didn't care. There were other priorities, even though her common sense told her one should be her job.

She phoned Kevin, brushing away all his questions about

absconding for days by telling him work was getting on top of her. She gave the same excuse to Tasha with all the intention of explaining that's why she had left work. She didn't want to admit she had been dismissed. She met with Kevin in bustling Ealing Broadway, and they sat inside Mama Lou's Coffee Bar where he ordered a cappuccino for himself, and sparkling water for her. He was dressed casually, jeans and a red jumper because he had been working from home. His smile was warm and love filled and she could see real appreciation for her in his eyes. This increased her guilt for what she was about to tell him.

'You okay, Honey? You don't look yourself.'

She didn't bother to pretend to smile, it would make no sense. 'I need to tell you something, Kev, something I only just discovered recently. I want you to understand that I had no idea about this, none whatsoever and I need you to believe me.'

Kevin reached out and took her hand. 'Of course I will. Honey, you need to know how I feel about you and—'

'Kev, please, just hear me out without interrupting.'

He folded his arms softly in listening mode and smiled warmly. 'Fire away, and don't look so worried, whatever haunts you I'll help you through it. Your mother tells me you've given up your job. You want me to put in a word for you at my company? We're always looking for good administrators.'

His good intentions brought tears to her eyes. 'I'm pregnant, Kev—'

He was up on his feet and pulling her into his arms before

she could say another word, his nose buried in her neck, his lips kissing her in a celebratory way. She felt sick, helpless.

'Kev, please, let's go, we need to talk,' She was removing his arms from around her and gathering her jacket and handbag, suddenly realising she had made a bad choice in choosing a public place like Mama Lou's Coffee bar to tell him such a devastating thing.

Kevin followed her, somewhat perplexed. He put a hand around her waist as they walked back to the car park in silence. Once in the car, she looked him squarely in the face.

'Honey, I'm not angry, this is the best news ever. Marry—'

Honey placed a finger to his lips, silencing him. 'I'm pregnant, but it's not yours.' She saw his confusion but kept going. 'At first when the doctor told me I was pregnant I thought it was yours... until he said I was fifteen weeks pregnant. If I was five or six weeks then it would have been yours. But fifteen weeks! Kev, it's not yours. I'm sorry. I didn't even know I was pregnant.' His devastation saturated the car and she pressed the window button to let it out before it broke her. Kevin stared out the window for a long time. She couldn't begin to guess at what was roaming his thoughts. She took to scaring herself, thinking that she didn't know him well enough and that he might try and hurt her, hit her even. She watched him carefully.

'I don't need to know who the father is, although I think I know,' he said flatly. 'But what do you want to do? Have you told him?'

She shook her head. 'Not yet, but I will.'

'You don't have to,' Kevin turned his head to look at her. 'I love you Honey. No-one has to know I'm not the real father. I can give you and your baby everything.'

She started crying and put her head on his shoulder. 'Oh, Kev, I couldn't live with that, not forever. The baby has a right to know their real father. I don't want to deceive anyone.'

'So, you're going to get back with him?'

She raised her head off his shoulder to look at him. 'No!' she cried, because she didn't want Ashley unless she was sure he loved her unconditionally and was over Bethany.

'So, what are you going to do?'

She returned her head to his shoulder. 'I don't know. I only just found out. I haven't had time to think. I only know I have to tell my mother, and of course... him.'

'You don't have to, Honey. Telling him will only complicate things. I'll be the father for your baby on paper, and I'll include this child and any other we have in my will.'

'I won't lie to a child about something as important as its father. Aaron isn't my real dad. I've known that from the start and I've been happy, but every now and then I wonder about my real father. I'd never tell Tasha this, but I do. So, I know how important it is to know your real parentage.'

'What about us? Where do we go from here?'

She wished she could give him the answer he wanted. 'I need to tell Tasha, and... him. After that I'll think about what I'm really going to do.'

'I don't want to lose you, Honey, I really don't. So just know I'm here for you, okay?'

She smiled wearily. 'Thanks, Kev.'

*

When she returned home from meeting with Kevin, Natasha was there to greet her. Feeling guilty, Honey insisted that she wanted to take her out for dinner, where she would have the perfect opportunity of breaking the news about her pregnancy. Ashley had introduced her to a nice Ethiopian restaurant in Cricklewood and she had always wanted to return.

They sat crossed legged on the beautiful patterned rug, facing each other over a small table with Natasha sipping Ethiopian fermented honey wine, and Honey an apple juice. The restaurant was small and intimate, decorated with sculptures and pictures from the Emperor Yohannes Dynasty. The largest was painted on goatskin and told the battle of Adowa, when Ethiopia rode to victory over the first Italian invasion. She could smell the coconut scent of the burning incense as the smoke snaked its way into her nostrils.

'I think this is quite exquisite,' Natasha commented, looking around her appreciatively. After the initial shock of having to take her high heels off, and sitting crossed legged on a mat, it was great to be having dinner alone with her daughter.

'Ashley used to bring me here. It's one of my favourite places, and you're my favourite lady.' She laughed at her mother's sceptic look. It was never easy trying to pull a fast one on Natasha, but she had to soften her towards Ashley. After all, he was the father-to-be of her unborn grandchild.

Love Again

'So, what do I really owe this pleasure to?'

Honey smiled sweetly. 'Can't a girl take her mother out? I just want you to know that I love you heaps.'

Natasha blew her a kiss. 'And I love you too. But what's the reason? You don't usually do these things without something in return.'

Honey held her eyes down. 'There is one thing I want to tell you... I'd better just come out and say it.' Honey placed her glass down on the table and found great comfort in staring at it and keeping her hand around it. 'I know you're going to cuss me and you're going to be vexed, and say I've ruined my life, but... I'm pregnant.' She braced herself for the torrents of "I told you so's" as she dared to raise her eyes to look at her silent mother.

Natasha hardly blinked. She smiled and sipped on her wine. 'You and Kevin will make wonderful parents. I know he'll ask you to marry him, that's if he hasn't already. You're twenty-nine—old and wise enough to be a mother. I'm happy for you. I'm looking forward to being a grandmother, although I'll never have a child call me that, you know. Any grandchildren can simply call me Tasha, just like their mother did.'

Honey looked puzzled. 'Is that it? Is that all you're going to say?'

'What more do you want me to say?'

'I thought you'd shout and give me a lecture or something, maybe take out a Fatwa on the father.'

Natasha smiled. 'I approve of Kevin, I'd never want any harm to come to him.'

'I know you do and I know you like him a great deal for a son-in-law,' Honey replied in sad honesty.

'Exactly!'

Honey viewed her mother suspiciously. 'You knew, didn't you Natasha Fontaine? You knew all this time that I was pregnant!'

'Not for sure, but yes. You hated the smell of everything, you slept at odd times, liked chunky chips, avocado and cucumber, sparkling water... dead giveaway... and now you order apple juice instead of your favourite wine, confirming my suspicion. I'm far from stupid, no matter what you might think.'

Honey draped an arm around her mother's shoulders. 'I know you're not stupid and I love you, Tasha—you're almost the best Mum a girl could have.' She placed a kiss on her mother's cheek. 'But there's one thing I have to tell you.' For the second time in the day she wondered about her choice of place to tell the news she was pregnant for Ashley Elliott. 'Tasha, I need to explain something to you, and I don't want you spitting like a cobra at me afterwards.'

Natasha looked puzzled. 'What?'

'I'm fifteen weeks pregnant. The implant failed and I didn't know because my periods don't really come often with the implants—'

'Fifteen weeks?' Natasha's voice was a whisper. 'Honey, fifteen weeks?' She sounded confused.

'Yes!' Honey snapped. 'It's Ashley's baby, not Kevin's.'

'My God!' Natasha's face was sucked into grief. 'Are you

203

serious? How could you be so stupid?'

Honey became defensive, her shoulders squaring up, her chin jaunting out. 'I'm twenty-nine years old, Tasha, not thirteen! Don't treat me like a child!'

Natasha heaved and took a sip of her drink. 'What's the father-to-be got to say? Will he marry you?'

Honey remained silent for a few moments, before answering part of the question. 'I haven't told him yet because I'm still reeling. I didn't want to be in this position.' As she finished her sentence, she wondered how truthful she really was.

'Does Kevin know?' Natasha asked curtly, unhappy at her daughter's naivety.

'Yes, I told him.'

'What did he say?'

'Kevin and I will sort this out, please don't push your nose in my business. Ashley never meant for me to get pregnant, but I have to let him know.'

'Yes, you do,' Natasha agreed. 'But everything that comes with his knowing, from now and for the next twenty years, will tie you together because of this child. Don't get any ideas about planting roots with this man, you'll probably end up a single mum.'

'I'll live with that, like you had to before daddy married you. Why do you hate him so much?'

'I don't. I just know he's uneasy in his own skin and it will eventually affect you.' Natasha sighed. 'One good thing out of this I guess, his bank balance is impressive.'

*

It took her most of the day to work up the courage to phone Ashley until she finally decided to drive round to his Kensington flat after 9pm. She knew that on a Tuesday he went home early, because it was the day he visited his mother, and after that he would always want to be alone. So, she sat in her car outside the gates and phoned him. He picked up on the second ring.

'Hon-Hon,' his voice sounded soaked in something sweet and sugary, like he was really pleased to hear from her and it made her heart skip. 'Nice, you calling me. Are you okay?' Concern suddenly crept into his voice.

'Yes, I'm fine. I'm outside your flat... now.'

There followed silence for a few seconds. 'Ashley, did you hear me?'

'Yes,' his voice now sounded uncertain. 'Why?'

'I need to talk to you.'

'Need? That's a strong word—'

'Are you going to open the fucking door or do I kick the shit down?' she snapped and heard him laugh.

'You been spending too much time with your Fatty, that's her thing. Okay, come in, I'm looking forward to the pleasure.'

The flat was like she remembered. Even down to the smell of the leather, marijuana and musky male cologne he smelled of. He was dressed only in his boxers and, by the smell of him, freshly showered. Her head reeled momentarily. She settled herself on the single sofa, her heart racing at knowing what her mouth must say.

'Want a drink?' He brought over the bottle of JD and two glasses.

Honey shook her head.

'Why the look?' he asked.

'What look?' she responded.

'The one on your face. What's wrong?'

She sighed and stared steadily at him.

'What I'm about to say still floors me. I mean, sometimes I think it's all a nightmare. But it hasn't gone away, and won't for some months.'

'You've got my interest,' he smiled serenely, loving the fact that she had chosen him to talk to about a problem in her life. Maybe she felt for him.

She looked at him sadly and he was suddenly afraid but didn't know why.

'Ash, you know that one night you and I had—'

'Girl, how can I forget! Three times in one night. You know what you did to me that night? I can't stop thinking about you. Do you know you have me like that? You've got me all—'

'I'm fifteen weeks pregnant and I thought you should know.'

Ashley didn't bother to drink from the glass that was on its way to his mouth. He placed it down and entwined his fingers. He stared hard at her for a whole minute or more before he finally spoke.

'Are you sure?' was all he found himself saying.

She just nodded. 'I was shocked too. I know how you feel, but I've had a week to deal with it and try to work out what I'm going to do.'

'And what exactly is that?' he asked in a voice she didn't know how to take.

'My first thing was to tell Kevin—'

'That guy your moms was trying to marry you off to? What has he got to do with anything?'

Honey was hesitant. 'It's awkward, Ashley. You and I had one night, Kevin and I had more nights but it just turned out that I was already pregnant and didn't know because the implant failed me. I'm going to keep the baby so I thought I should let you know. I know—'

'How nice of you to consider telling me.' The sarcasm was blatant.

'Well, we're nothing to each other—'

Ashley cut in. 'Nothing to each other but we've created a real human life, right? You're going to have my baby but we're nothing to each other and I don't have a say in anything?'

'What kind of say do you want?'

Ashley stood up to face her. 'I don't know yet. I don't have a clue about being a father or what that means or what I'm supposed to do.'

Honey turned away and walked to the door. 'I have a scan next Thursday at Queen Charlotte Hospital at 2pm, call me if you'd like to come.' She opened the door and looked back at him, suddenly feeling sorry for the scared little boy he looked like. 'You don't have to be a part of this if it makes you uncomfortable, I can do this myself.'

He didn't respond because, in a way, he hoped she could.

Twenty-Three

Dame arrived at A One Studio at 8:30am, in time to set things up for the first appointment an hour later. As he entered, he disarmed the alarm and walked down the spacious hall leading to the X room. Ashley was there, standing quite still, his face pressed against the glass looking out of the window, his hands buried in his pockets. He walked over and stood beside Ashley, his arms crossed in front of him.

'You know, Ash,' Dame moved one hand to place a finger at the corner of his mouth in thought mode, 'I think you'd feel better if you just call her.'

Ashley squeezed his eyes closed and placed each hand on his temples. His stomach growled, reminding him that he hadn't eaten. In fact, he hadn't been eating properly for the past few days since Honey told him her news. He lowered his hands and his shoulders drooped.

'Hon's pregnant, Dame.'

'She didn't do it by herself, I think she had some help. How's she doing?'

Ashley walked towards the sofas. He flopped down, but not before grabbing a can of beer off the table. He pulled back the loop to open it and its contents bubbled up and snaked down the tin onto the laminate floor before he could get it to his mouth. He drank thirstily, only now realising that he was thirsty. He leaned back casually, his legs apart.

'She doesn't seem to want much to do with me—says she has some scan soon, and I can come if I want. I mean, she drops a bomb like that and it seems I have no say.'

'It's the woman's body, mate.' Dame walked and sat upright on the opposite sofa, pulling a bunch of tissue out of the box on the table to mop up Ashley's spill.

Ashley nodded. 'I know. I know. I can't let her go, man. I've been wanting her for so long, one night's all I got with her. And now she's going to have a baby—'

'Your baby,' Dame pointed a finger. 'Your flesh and blood.'

'My baby. My baby.' Ashley threw his head back and took another gulp of beer, swirling it around his mouth before swallowing. 'That's scary shit I tell you, scary shit. I mean what the fuck do I know about being a father? I only remember bad things about my old man.'

'That's good, because then you won't do the things he did and you'll be a better Dad.'

'You think so?' Ashley squeezed the now empty can with one hand. He hoped so.

'Yeah, I reckon.'

'When Bethany betrayed me, I didn't want to love again. I was okay on my own. Then I saw Hon.'

Dame got up to get a beer out of the fridge. He wiped the top with the sleeve of his shirt before opening it and pouring it into a long, slim glass. 'Did you tell Honey about Beth?'

'No. Why should I? Hon isn't even serious about me. The only reason I'm back on her grid is because she's pregnant. She'd make a good mom though.'

'Yes. And you would make a good father.'

'I don't know about that,' Ashley responded.

'Well, I do. I've watched you father your mother and your little sister. I'm not saying this because we're second cousins, you've done good by those two women in your life and you can do good by Honey. Not all women get bored and do the dirty on you.'

Ashley was having some serious internal battles, mostly with his conscience. The urge was strong to call her, park up outside her house, but she hadn't called him either and was acting like she didn't need him, and he had to admit that she didn't. Not with her supportive parents, and not with Kevin around.

He eventually called her a day later, the longest day of his life since his mother's breakdown, and her voice was unwelcoming, which wasn't new.

'So, why have you called?'

Ashley looked at the phone in his hand before returning it to his ear.

'Can I see you so we can talk, please? I'll come and pick you up now, if it's convenient for you,' he added.

Ashley arrived at Honey's Ealing home at breakneck speed, just as she was walking out of the front door wearing a fitted black and white jersey dress. His eyes immediately went to her middle where signs that she was pregnant were not obvious, unless you knew what you were looking for. He turned off the music, irritated by the moving curtains of her neighbours and he truly hoped him driving into their idyllic little cul-de-sac lowered the prices of their homes. Honey opened the passenger door and got in, reaching for the seat belt to clip snuggly around her body.

Ashley drove without speaking. He kept his music too loud for any conversation to take place as Honey sat on both hands, enjoying the music and getting lost in a world of signs as she watched the motorway whiz past, wondering where he was taking her. She wasn't going to ask or be the first one to break the silence so she closed her eyes and after a while succumbed to the hum of the engine lulling her into sleep.

She opened her eyes and looked around sleepily. The car was parked and she did not recognise her surroundings.

'We're in Barns,' he answered her puzzled look.

'Why?'

'It's where my moms live.'

She looked startled.

'Well, I figured if she's going to be a grandma, she'd better meet the moms of the child.'

Honey was not amused. She pursed her lips together disapprovingly and folded her arms.

'What?' Ashley pinched her nose and she was amazed he could be so playful at such a time. Didn't he understand their predicament?

'I would've wanted time to dress properly. I can't meet

your mother like this. And what are we going to tell her? There's nothing between us, this baby was an accident. You've been living your life and I've been living mine.'

Ashley smiled at her frustration, how good it looked on her. Her slightly flushed caramel skin, two red spots appearing on her cheeks, an indication he knew meant anger or desire.

'We're here now and she has as much right as Natatrash— does she know I'm the father of her first grandchild?'

'Ashley, you piss me off—'

'I know, but we're here now, and my moms is as important to me as yours is to you, so if she's about to become a grandmother she has a right to know.'

He saw her protest melt away in the movement of her shoulders and was gripped momentarily by panic. He was about to introduce Honey to his mother. Beloved as she was, she was mentally scarred, and he didn't know how she would react to the news of becoming a grandmother. He was hoping it might change her direction of self-destructive thoughts.

When he popped to the home yesterday his mother was in good spirits, but that's no indication that normality would still be there today. His mother remained half a person, living between two worlds, or even more, as far as he could see. He'd told Honey that his mother had a breakdown after his father left, but he hadn't told her that she was still broken and lived in a shelter.

He got out of the car and opened the passenger door, holding out a hand to assist her, still wondering if he'd done the right thing. Had he given enough thought to how his mother would react to meeting someone new? How she would react to the news, when she may associate pregnancy with the darkest time in her life? She was prone to terrible mood swings and hallucinations, always ending with her thinking he was his father, and pleading with him to come home. After all these years, she hadn't recovered from being rejected and abandoned, and after all these years he still hated his father.

'She lives here?' Honey's tone matched her shocked expression. He held her hand and they walked the few yards to the front door, a strong smell of lavender drifting over them from the lined pathway. A small Chinese man opened the door, his face breaking into a toothless smile at the sight of Ashley. He stepped back for them to enter.

'Hallo, Ash. I'm Brad Pitt today!' He jumped up and down, clapping his small hands. 'Your mam cooked us some curry goat. I never had that before. I'm Brad Pitt!'

'That's nice, Brad.' Ashley patted his shoulder in a friendly way. 'Where's my Moms?'

'She's in the living room. She's good today.'

Ashley beckoned to Honey to follow him down the corridor. He breathed a little easier at hearing she was in a good mood. That meant she must have been agreeable about taking her medication and her daily bath. Honey entered the large room and noted the naked walls, high ceiling and huge bay windows that led out to a very green, well-maintained lawn. It lacked personality, Honey thought. It was like an immaculate shell, filled only with the loneliness of its inhabitants. Honey's heart went out to the lost soul sitting on the deep green fabric sofa, staring unseeingly into space.

'Moms, how's it going?' Ashley asked cautiously, gently. 'I brought a friend to meet you. Her name is Honey.'

Honey smiled nervously. 'Hi.'

Ashley sat with care beside his mother. She turned her head slowly and a smile of recognition erupted on her face.

'Elliott?' Her trembling hand touched his face. Ashley held onto her hand and kissed it. Honey swallowed a lump.

'No Moms, it's me, Ash.'

Disappointment briefly crossed her face. 'Oh, Ash, you look so like your father.'

Honey saw the flash of annoyance ignite his face. He didn't like talking about his father. When she'd asked about him once, he'd told her never to mention him again. She was curious to know why his hatred ran so deep, but it wasn't unusual. Many people she knew didn't get on with their fathers or even know them, including herself.

'Who have you got there?' She looked past him to Honey.

'This is Honey, my friend, er, special friend.'

Honey's heart skipped. She was in denial as to why.

'Come here, girl,' his mother beckoned.

Honey sat on the other side of her.

'So,' she held Honey's hand, 'you are the one. I've never met any of Ash's girlies. You must be special. I'm Doreen, but you can call me Dee.' She smiled.

Honey could see that, although Dee's body had been wrecked by medication and her mind emptied of reality, she'd been a real beauty at one time in her life. Her black hair intertwined with grey, though short and unkempt, was full bodied and would look a world of difference with a wash and blow. Her eyes were blue, her skin pale, ashy and wrinkled, but considering the stress she'd endured it was understandable. 'Ash always comes to see me. He's a good one. What special occasion brought you here today?'

Ashley's eyes darted to Honey's belly. Dee's calm demeanour ebbed away as horror took over her face. Ashley quickly moved in.

'It's okay, Moms—'

Dee stood up, shaking her head frantically. 'No, it's not. Don't leave her Ash, don't kill her heart. Promise me—'

Ashley put a firm comforting arm around her shoulders, trying to encourage her to sit. 'It's okay, Moms. I won't leave her, don't worry.'

Dee breathed a sigh of relief and allowed Ashley to seat her again. 'Good boy,' she squeezed his hands, tearfully. 'Not like your Dad, you're a good boy. What do you want, a girl or a boy?' She smiled, her outburst seconds earlier already forgotten.

Honey hoped her smile wasn't as visibly tight as it felt being stretched across her lips, which she felt were trembling.

'I don't mind, a boy—'

'It's a girl!' Ashley cut in. 'A pretty baby girl, like you,' he hugged his mother and stroked her hair like he was the father and she was the child.

Honey sat silently watching. The way he brushed at a stubborn stain on his mother's sleeve and kept smoothing down her hair. Honey understood more now; he had his own childhood trauma to deal with. She felt a deep sadness for Dee because the love of her life had obviously destroyed her. Honey was now grateful for her upbringing and understood better her mother's fear for her. Because Natasha knew first-hand about heart-break and rejection, and what it could do to the human spirit. Looking at Dee it was all so obvious.

Twenty-Four

September 2016

Fatty, Honey and Zhara sat crossed legged on Honey's bed eating Häagen-Dazs ice cream and cashew nuts—Honey's latest craving. She changed position, using the pillows against the headboard to prop herself up. She had filled the girls in on her meeting with Ashley's mother, about seeing a tender, protective side of him.

'I tell you,' Honey scooped a full spoon of ice cream into her mouth, 'it was really amazing seeing that side of him. He's proper caring.'

Fatty wasn't carried away by the enthusiasm. 'Jack the Ripper was proper caring to his mother, that don't say anything about his character.'

Zhara, her chin resting on her fist, gave her input. 'I don't know, Ash is a real conundrum. Since Bethany slept with his business competition, no other woman has been able to bed him. Ash was crazy about her, she shouldn't have messed up like that and got found out. Me, if I ever go on the down low and get found out, I'm denying it... even if he thought he saw me with his own eyes, I'll be cussing him about his lying eyes! You never admit!'

'I never knew you had that in you, Za. I always thought you were the classic-man-push-over.' Zhara had Fatty's attention in a way she had never before.

'Read my lips, I ain't admitting to anything! Beth is a fool, and now she's a broke fool coz Ash ain't spending on her anymore.' Zhara laughed.

'Yeah, the problem with Beth is she, like most beautiful, stunning women, think she can have her cake and eat it.'

Bethany had been like a ghost to Honey, a ghost she hadn't given much thought to. She didn't even know what Bethany looked like. And she didn't want to.

'Guess what?' Fatty was changing the subject. 'I hear Ahmed's girlfriend has gone on the run in some women's refuge. Did you know, Za? He must have been beating the shit out of her... like he did his wife, that's why she left his arse, taking their three kids.' Fatty shivered involuntarily. 'God, how do we make you see, Za?'

'She sees but she just thinks it can't happen to her,' Honey said.

Zhara stood up agitated, her fists clenched as she glared at her friends sitting cross-legged on the bed.

'I don't know that side of him, okay—'

'Yet,' Fatty butted in, 'but you're gonna wait to taste his fists, right? Only then you'll believe—when he kills you.'

Zhara took a step closer to them on the bed. 'Ahmed isn't abusing her. He only got mad because she's threatening him with the police. Our Somali men are proud—you tell them about police, of course they'll beat your shit.'

'And that's cool?' Fatty snapped. 'For fuck's sake Za, you're being so fucking blind. If he can beat his wife and mother of his children, and beat that dumb girl he shacked up with, then he can certainly beat his bit on the side—you!'

Zhara shook her shoulders as if dislodging an object. 'You know what your moms always says, Honey?' She turned her glare to Honey. 'She always says "A ghost knows who to frighten," and that's it with Ahmed. He wouldn't dare raise his hands to me.'

'Stupid bitch.' Fatty said flippantly. 'Anyway, I just want to concentrate on my wedding and Hon's baby. Your baby will be here before my wedding, so I guess me and stupid Za here will have to organise your baby shower.'

'That's ages yet.' Honey scooped her last spoon of ice cream into her mouth.

'Not so,' Fatty was adamant. 'You're six months gone. Let's make some plans for your baby and my wedding.' She reached for Honey's laptop on the desk. 'Let's look at some wedding dresses. What do you think if I get married in pink?'

Honey wrinkled her nose. Zhara screeched.

'Who are you? Barbie?' Za asked in exaggerated amazement.

Fatty laughed. 'Good God, I don't want my wedding to be compared to Barbie! But I do want an unforgettable wedding dress. They say you only wear a wedding dress once, but I want to wear mine twice... my wedding and my funeral.'

'Don't talk about your wedding and funeral in one sentence,' Honey scolded, 'it's not a good omen.'

Fatty concealed the urge to laugh; Natasha would have pointed something out like that.

'Well, I don't believe in omens. What about a date for your baby shower? You ain't got long. What about Kevin, what's he saying?'

Honey looked uncomfortable. 'Kev says he'll be here for me and the baby, but he doesn't want Ashley to have any input.'

'Who the fuck does he think he is? Just because he's got a few bucks, he wants to tell you what to do with your own baby? Well serves him right, Ash's bank balance is possibly ten times his. Let him fuck off!'

Honey had been tempted to tell Kevin just that, only stopping because of the respect she had for him and the fact that he was a really nice guy. She knew how hurt and disappointed he was that it wasn't his baby, and that, despite this, he was still willing to make things work, even going as far as trying to suggest marriage.

'At the moment, I'm avoiding both their calls.'

'Truth is Hon,' Fatty said laughing, 'you got the advantage here. You've got Kevin wanting to save face by marrying you and pretending the baby's his, and you got Ash trying to send you on a guilt trip,' she broke off to laugh again. 'You're lucky that both of them can give your baby a really good life.'

*

Over the next couple of weeks, Honey never regretted anything more than she regretted losing her job. Sat at home watching daytime television with the same regurgitated male and female presenters was near to driving her mad, and she couldn't fathom how people stayed home, couldn't understand how anyone could settle for a life without meaning. Each day she channel hopped from station to station on the television, and watched the clock until her father's key turned in the door. She would greet him in the hall, extracting from him details of his journey home and his day at work. She then repeated the same thing an hour later when her mother arrived home.

'You're bored,' Natasha told her as Honey met her in the hall on Thursday evening, taking the plastic carrier bag containing fruits out of her hand. 'You need a job.'

Honey laughed as she looked down on her bump, now showing through her clothes. 'Who's going to employ me in this state?' she asked, and didn't really need an answer as the tell-tale sign of interference registered on her mother's face.

A week later, before Natasha could interfere with finding her work, Honey secured herself a job from Dorota, the stunning, young Polish woman on the fruit and veg stall in Shepherd's Bush Market. She was mostly kept busy selling super cheap fruits and vegetables, £5 could easily give you two carrier bags full, and the customers came fast and plenty. Honey was glad for the distraction and loved the interaction with so many different people. She gathered stories from people who had come from Egypt, Tanzania, Peru, Ireland, even Nepal. It amazed her how they even thought to come to this little borough of West London. How did they choose Shepherd's Bush? The smiles and the stories from her customers were her true reward, despite Natasha giving her grief about working on a market stall with her first-class Communications and English degree. Honey was not surprised to be assisted by a pair of large, capable hands as she picked up a small crate of tomatoes. He took the crate firmly out of her hands.

'What are you doing?' Kevin's frown was stark. 'Your mother told me you were working here and I couldn't believe it. Why? You know I'll—'

'Kev, hi—so sorry Tasha had to drag you into this. Look, I have another customer so I'll talk to you later.'

Kevin stood, obstructing the customer who had approached the stall.

'Excuse me,' a small Chinese woman tapped Kevin's back. 'I want serve now; you move so I get serve.'

Honey leaned to one side to see Mrs Fung, one of the regulars. Just then, Dorota came back with two paper cups of hot chocolate, giving Honey one.

'Honey, really? Is this what you want to do with your life?' Kevin indicated the stall with his hand. 'A little fruit and veg sales person?'

Dorota looked at him and then at Honey with an amusing query across her brow.

'Kev, I have lunch in an hour so I can talk—'

'No, no, go take your lunch now,' Dorota shooed her. 'I'll take over this little fruit and veg stall.'

'Good,' Mrs Fung said, 'I not like him; he blocked my

fruits and vegetables, he talk rude at Honee.' She gave Kevin a shove, which did next to nothing to move him but left him looking quite bewildered.

They sat in Kevin's car because he had parked on double yellow.

'I told you before that if you want work, I can fix something up for you. Why are you working on a market stall?'

Honey was annoyed now. 'You offended me and Dorota and our customers. I didn't know you were such a snob, Kev. You got a lot in common with Tasha. What does it matter where I work, as long as I enjoy it and get paid?'

'You can't possibly enjoy working in the freezing cold—'

'It's not freezing,' Honey pointed out.

'Maybe not today, but it's still cold.'

'I don't really feel it that much,' she lied. 'I think it must have something to do with me being pregnant,' she said, knowing he wouldn't have a clue. 'And for the record, I feel really insulted the way you say 'market stall', like it's a dirty word.'

Kevin reached for her hands and rubbed them between his. 'Your hands are cold,' he said, 'and soon they'll be rough and dirty with grime.'

Honey withdrew her hands and rubbed them together. 'I do wash this dirt and grime off at some point, you know. Look, Kev. Thanks for the offer of work, but this is just a temp thing. I want to keep my mind busy and save some money for the baby—'

'I told you that I'd take care of—'

'And I told you that I want to do something too. I'm not useless, and I may think a thousand pounds is a lot of money, because it is for me, but don't try and shove your ethos on me because I'll just think you're trying to bully and control me.'

Kevin looked crushed. 'Please, Honey, never, ever think that way about me. I want the best for you. I—are you still seeing him?' He looked pained.

'You mean Ashley? No, I'm not *seeing* him, not in that way. He does call me.'

'Look, Honey, I can give you and your baby everything. You'll have a place to live, if you want, we can employ a nanny, I can finance your dream of your own publishing company, get you the best business advisors, just tell me what you want.'

'And remind me again,' Honey looked alert, 'what do you want?'

'You know what I want. I want you as my wife. I want to marry you, but I want you to promise that you'll never see this other man again. I'll take care of everything you and your baby need.'

For the rest of the afternoon, Honey was deep in thought. Kevin still didn't seem to get that the way he presented things was very instructional, in a controlling way. His offer was tempting though, to have all her financial needs met, all her baby would ever want. It was tempting, and she couldn't wait to talk to Fatty and Zhara about it. An hour before it was time to pack up, Honey looked up to serve her next customer and saw Ashley's smiling face, his amber eyes warm and friendly.

'What are you grinning at?' Honey couldn't help returning

his friendly smile.

'Just shocked to see you standing in Shepherd's Bush Market selling fruits and veg. You've impressed me again, Hon-Hon.'

'Why?' Honey was genuinely pleased to hear she had impressed him.

'I love how you just get on with things, you know. How's my baby?' He pointed to her bulge, 'you're looking all sexy and round.'

'If you mean fat, I'm supposed to gain weight during pregnancy.'

'Don't be so offended, I think you look gorge. Can we talk quickly?'

Honey glanced at Dorota, who was serving a customer. Without a breath, Dorota responded.

'Off you go. It's quietened down now so you might as well go home. I must say you're popular today, and I like this one better,' she winked.

Honey was tired and refused Ashley's offer of dinner at the club, so he drove her straight home along the Uxbridge Road into Ealing.

'It's been a long day for me. I start at 5:00am and to be honest after lunch I'm usually ready for a nap. Only the customers keep me bubbling. I feel good about myself.'

'So you should. I feel good about you too.'

They looked at each other and laughed, and Honey resented going inside her house because she knew the spell would be broken, and she would be filled with the familiar doubts.

Before she could open the door, he placed his hand gingerly on her bump and she held her breath as the warmth penetrated her tee shirt. Her stomach jerked and Ashley withdrew his hand in instant shock. Honey laughed, pulling his hand back.

'It's been kicking for a while,' she smiled. 'It's a really strange feeling at first, you know. It's like something else lives in your body. It's strange but it's nice.'

Ashley gently rubbed her stomach, smiling at the thought that it was his baby moving around.

'What's the due date?' he asked.

'December 25th if it comes on time.' Then she decided to tell him her dilemma, to see if he had any suggestions. 'Kevin's asked me to marry him.' She saw his face contort but he still kept up his gentle massage of her stomach. 'He says he'll give us, me and the baby, everything we need—'

'I'll provide for my child, Hon-Hon, of that you can be sure. I can't stand the thought of that—'

'Ashley,' Honey's voice was soft as she cut him off. 'Since finding out about being pregnant, I haven't slept with Kevin, okay? I haven't and I won't until after the baby.'

'Then you'll start sleeping with him again?'

'It depends on what you have to offer, Ashley. I read somewhere that Bob Marley said a man has no right playing with a woman's love, if he has no good intentions of loving her back.'

Twenty-Five

October 2016

Ashley got the unexpected call from his brother at 4am. He couldn't really believe that his brother was calling to tell him that their father had had a stroke. What did it have to do with him, Ashley had asked Nathan, who pleaded with him to see sense. "There's so much more to what you don't know," Nathan told him. It didn't matter, he knew all he needed to, saw the proof every week on his visits to his moms.

It took a couple days of badgering phone calls from Nathan before Ashley agreed to go and see his father. Hours of Nathan's pleading and begging finally made Ashley relent and he promised to stay for two days. Marley wore him down too, when he eventually told her about their sick father. She wanted to see the man who left because of her, who made her mother hate her so much.

Nathan picked them up at O'Hare Airport in Illinois, and drove them to the home of their father, a four up, four down house with a two-bed basement in which their father lived. It shocked them both, the state their father was in. The state their father lived in. The space was certainly big enough, the lounge was twice the size of Ashley's and the kitchen, bedrooms and bathrooms were not far behind. The lounge contained three sets of three-seater sofas, all worn and stained, while the curtain's true colours were not obvious. Under his feet, the chipped wooden floor was partially covered by a mat that may have been patterned at one time. Similarly worn down, Ashley finally gazed at the man who had walked out on his family all those years ago. That man had been tall, athletic and handsome, with a laugh that was bellowing and infectious. Now, that man was withered, gaunt and limp, sitting in a wheelchair. His father's dead eyes brightened, like a light had been beamed into them, when Nathan pointed and said: 'Look, Elliott, that's Ash. Your boy's come to see you. And that's Marley, the baby girl Moms had.'

Ashley and Marley stood rooted in awkwardness by the living room door. Ashley came equipped with the venom of betrayal, rejection, and anger, for all the years he'd been left alone to save his mother's life and father his sister. It was a job his father should have done, a job he ran out on. Ashley felt mad to find him living in such dire conditions, to be sitting in a wheelchair looking like he wasn't long for this world.

'This is what you left us for?' he asked the stranger sitting in the wheelchair.

The light left his father's eyes and his speech was incomprehensible, just grunts and a pathetic noise, like a wounded bear.

'What's wrong with him?' Ashley turned to Nathan.

'Been getting strokes and all them shit, can't talk or move all that side of him,' Nathan pointed at his father's right arm. 'And he's diabetic. He's in a real mess, Ash, that's why he wanted to see you and Marley. I'm sure he wanted to say sorry, that's why I wanted you to come sooner. But the last stroke he had took his speech. He's been suffering, Ash, real bad.'

Ashley felt sick to the guts because he was secretly moved as he watched his father. 'So, where's his woman?'

'Who? That fucking gold-digger? She's living upstairs and she's rented out the middle floor to a family. She put Dad down here and only comes to see if he's still alive... she's got this so called nurse who gives him his needles and feeds him liquidised food three times a day and cleans him... the bitch is just waiting for him to die so she can have it all, Ash, but what she don't know is he's left it all for us, his kids, Marley and Moms.'

Ashley took a few hesitant steps further into the room. Marley followed him. He wasn't quite sure what the colour of the walls were either, everything seemed so dingy.

'It's called justice.' For some reason Ashley couldn't go too close to his father. 'Look at you,' Ashley dropped his shoulders, releasing his rucksack onto the floor. 'Was she worth it? You left Moms pregnant... you left us—'

Nathan took Ashley by the shoulders. 'Easy, bruv, the old man's fragile... he got blood pressure problems too, you don't want to cause him to stroke out again.'

'I don't care, he had it coming.' Ashley shrugged Nathan off and took steps to stand before his father, whose mouth only emitted distorted sounds.

'I only come here for two things. To tell you what I think about you, and to punch your head in. You know Moms cracked after you left her eight months pregnant with my sister?' He pointed to a tearful Marley standing behind him. 'She cracked and never, ever healed. All she thinks about, even now, is you, and that one day you'll go back to her. You think she wants your death money? She'd rather have had a husband. You didn't even make one phone call. Not one! You didn't send us no birthday cards, or even a picture so that we could know that we had a father. I wish Moms could see you now, see that she's been wasting her life loving you.'

Maybe it was a way of punishing himself, or maybe it was a journey into finding and understanding himself, but Ashley found himself becoming his father's carer over the next ten days. He extended his stay. He stayed and fixed up the place in that short space of time. He had it painted and new furniture put in. He hired a new private nurse to care for his father and wondered why Nathan, who lived three blocks down in a luxury condo, hadn't done it before. After all, it was Nathan who felt more empathy, who was always pushing for a reunion, it would've made more sense if he'd taken care of his father. But Nathan, as Ashley discovered, was all about Nathan. And Nathan, Ashley saw for himself, had a warped concept of responsibility. After that first day of delivering them to their father, it was a whole week before they saw him again. Nathan took nothing seriously. His only true love was money. He talked a good talk, but it really was just do as I say, not as I do. Ashley loved his brother despite it all, and Nathan loved Ashley.

'You're made of good stuff, bro,' Nathan told him over a game of dominoes around the dining room table as Marley tended to their father in the bedroom. 'I don't know what would've become of Dad if you didn't stay and fix everything up. I couldn't look after him.'

'You mean you didn't want to.'

Nathan had the decency to look guilty. 'I'm not like you, Ash, and you're not like me. I'm like the old man,' he flicked his head towards the bedroom. 'Before he took sick, he lived to have the time of his life with the three W's. Women, wine, and weed... that was him. And as for his bitch, she does the same things he does.'

Ashley studied the dominoes he held in each hand, he had four remaining to Nathan's two. Ashley watched his brother's eager fingers as they tapped on the table, and his eyes fixed on the dominoes in his other hand.

'That's what he left us for? That kind of life?' He threw down a double six and knew by the way Nathan tightened his lips that he would have to pass.

'Pass,' Nathan said. 'Our Pa is a hunter, Ash, like me... all men are hunters, that's what we're naturally good at. Moms tells me you're going to have a baby. What's baby mama say about you being out here away from her?'

Ashley banged the domino on the table. 'I didn't tell her.'

Nathan rubbed his chin, two lines formed across his fore-head. 'What d'you mean you didn't tell her?'

Ashley answered with force. 'She's involved with someone else.'

Nathan considered this for less than a second before moving on. 'I know Dad fucked up, he cheated on our Moms a whole lot, that natural hunting instinct again, but you gotta know there's always two sides to a story, and the truth sits in the middle. Moms wasn't innocent in all this Ash, and I'm hoping you're old enough to be able to handle what I'm about to tell you.'

Ashley's face immediately caved into a frown. 'What do you think I've been handling since I was ten years old, Nate?'

Nathan viewed him with a seriousness Ashley had never seen.

'Marley,' Nathan whispered. 'She ain't Dad's.'

Ashley stared at his brother, not daring to blink or listen to Nathan's answer to the question he was about to ask.

'What did you say?' Ashley's voice was tight and cold, filled with disbelief.

'Dad was a hunter, but Moms started hunting too. You won't remember, but I do. You were about four years old when it all started. Moms was always dressing up and smelling good, and she kicked Dad out of their bedroom. He was sleeping on the sofa, Ash. Don't you remember?'

'You're lying. Why would you lie on our Moms like that?' Confusion seeped in as an image took shape: a memory of his father sitting on the sofa in the mornings, bare chested but in pyjama pants, sipping from a cup, which his gaze was always focused on, as if trying to avoid eye contact with anyone.

Nathan leaned towards Ashley. 'I wouldn't tell a lie like that, Ash. I love our moms too, but she got pregnant, and Dad didn't want no part of it and it pissed her off so much she went mental. I feel for Marley, but we can't tell her. Dad said I shouldn't tell a soul, especially not you, with you loving Moms so much, but I don't want to be lumbered with such a secret on my own.'

A pain split his heart at the thought of Marley and this new revelation. He could hardly believe his mother's suffering was her own doing, that she had been just like Bethany, the *devil* in the details. Still, it made no difference, he hated his father. If his mother had become a hunter, it was because his father taught her.

'You believe what that lying bastard tells you about our moms! You believe him? He's a liar—'

'Yeah, he is, but not about this. I was older than you, Ash. I saw things. I knew Moms was seeing other men, different men. You were too young to even understand what you saw.'

The house phone rang and Nathan walked over to answer it. The way his face changed told Ashley it wasn't good news. After placing down the receiver, he turned to Ashley.

'It's not good, bruv,' he hung up the phone, his face distressed. 'It's not good.'

Ashley stood up slowly, wiping the tears away. 'What?'

'That was Mrs Reece, trying to get hold of you. Moms... she hung herself and left you a note saying she was going home.'

*

Ashley had been on automatic when he organised the full-time nursing care for his father, while still feeling conflicted and gripped by grief at the loss of his mother. What Nathan revealed about Marley had numbed him, and finding out his beloved mother had gone in such a terrible way, he was kept going only by avoiding all thoughts like objects being thrown at him. All that mattered now was Marley, Honey and his baby. That new thought sprouted hope like seeds. He could get through this, he had to.

When they arrived back in London, Marley and Nathan went directly to Auntie Dawn. Ashley was in a sombre mood as he entered the house where his mother had spent her last years. The note was in her recognisable scribble: *Going home now, Ash*. He held it to his cheek and sobbed, feeling that all the things Nathan had accused their mother of would remain unchallenged forever. In this moment of torture and anguish, he could only think of Honey. He phoned her, but his call went unanswered.

Honey was in Bath on a weekend break with Kevin, at one of the spa hotels, when she saw the missed call from Ashley, and immediately called him back. His distress was evident. Everything negative she thought about him previously dissolved in that moment as she listened to his pained voice gasping, stuttering that his beloved mother was dead.

'Can I see you now, Hon-Hon? Will you come? Please.'

'Of course. I'm in Bath, but I'll make my way back now,'

she said, making unwavering eye contact with Kevin so that he was clear about her determination.

'Was that him?' Kevin asked glumly once she was off the phone.

'Yes, that was Ashley. His mother has died.'

'Excuse my ignorance, and condolences to him, but what has that got to do with you?'

Honey shook her head. 'Kev, how can you be so unfeeling at a time like this? The man's mother, his world as far as I can see, has just died. He's devastated.'

'So why call you? Doesn't he have anyone else to call?'

Honey shrugged. It was a good question. Ashley must have hordes of people he could call at a time like this, and maybe he had done so already, but he had still chosen to call her.

'You told me there was never anything serious between you two, has anything changed?' Kevin pushed.

'The man's mother has just died, Kev. His mother and my unborn child's grandmother, maybe that's why he called. It doesn't matter,' she said, getting up from the table, 'I need to get back to London tonight.'

'I'll take you first thing in the morning if I must, but not tonight. May I remind you that I booked two rooms, at your insistence, and they don't come cheap?'

'Then I'll get a taxi, train or bus, but I'm going tonight and I'll pay you back for my room.'

Kevin watched her with stern eyes, but eventually surrendered.

'Let's not argue about him, and of course I don't expect

you to pay me back for the room. Let's get our bags and head out. We could get back into London by nine, if the traffic is light.'

Kevin insisted on dropping Honey off and collecting her from Ashley's house, and an argument broke out.

'Am I wasting my time here, Honey?' Kevin snapped. 'I've put it all on the table for you. I'm willing to bring up another man's child because I love you, but you don't seem to know your mind. Is there any hope for us? Me and you?'

'Kev, if this baby was yours,' Honey placed a hand on her stomach, 'there wouldn't be a problem. I can't commit to you the way you want right now; all I can tell you is that I like you a lot and I enjoy your company—that hasn't changed.'

'Can you do me a favour?' Kevin asked.

Honey nodded.

'Don't sleep with him, please. Promise me.'

'Kev! I won't promise anything of the sort. I've already told you, Ashley and I don't have that kind of relationship.'

'But one phone call from him brings you at breakneck speed to his aid... you say one thing about him, but do another.'

'I'm not asking you to wait on me or anything like that, Kevin—'

'I know you're not. It would be good for me if you did ask, because I know I can love you more than he ever can. I'm serious about you, Honey, and I want us to sort something permanent out before the baby comes.'

'That's less than two months, don't rush me, please.'

She got out of his car and jumped straight into hers,

driving off as she saw her mother open the front door and walk hurriedly towards Kevin's car.

Ashley had on grey jogging bottoms and a black vest. His even shaped dreadlocks were loose, falling past his shoulders. His eyes were sad and haunted. She walked in and closed the door behind her. He took her into his arms immediately and she hugged him back as they stood perfectly still in their embrace.

'She's gone, Hon-Hon. She left a note saying she was going home.'

Honey gently pulled out of his arms and led him by the hand into the living room, guiding him down on the sofa and sitting beside him, still holding his hand.

'I'm so sorry, Ashley.'

'I always thought that one day she would come back home. I bought her a new house. I would've given her the world, if only she would get better. Now it's too late, she's gone. Gone.' He lowered his head and gently rested his cheek against Honey's bump as he sobbed. She stroked his hair silently because she knew there would be no words to comfort him for such a loss.

When his sobs had subsided and he had disappeared into the bathroom to wash his face, she poured him a drink and made herself some hot chocolate. It was strange seeing him so vulnerable, she thought as he walked back towards her on the sofa, thanking her for the drink.

'I forgot the headache crying can give.' His self-effacing smile was sad. 'She hung herself with the sheets from her bed,' he croaked, 'taking a library of secrets with her. My brother told me that Marley doesn't belong to our dad, that Moms didn't know who Marley belonged to... All the time I thought the old man had run out on her for some young bimbo, and that's what had caused her breakdown. But Nate says different. He says our moms was a player, a hunter, and had lots of problems. I can never tell Marley the truth.'

'Why not? I think she deserves to know.'

'What would it solve? Maybe if we knew who her real father was, but we don't have a clue. Our moms never loved Marley, and now I understand why. I just thought her dislike was because our dad left her pregnant, and she couldn't handle it. I wish she was here to answer some of my questions. I don't understand why she would do what Nate says she was doing.'

'What do you remember from your childhood?' Honey asked.

'Moms always trying to kill herself and me always coming just in time,' he delivered dismally.

'What about before she was sick? Don't you remember good times?'

He smiled, a faraway sad smile. 'Yes. She paid for my piano lessons because she loved to listen to me play. I remember that she always smelt good, her perfume was Eternity—she loved that, and I remember Dad taking me shopping to buy it for a Mother's Day present. I just can't remember when it all started going bad for them. I just woke up one morning and Dad had slept on the sofa and kept doing so until he left us.'

'And you blamed him for your mother's breakdown?'

'Yes. She changed when he left, what was I supposed to think? I was ten years old and my mother lost herself and never came back. All she would talk about was him coming back. I think she replaced her love for him with the church. She started going nearly every day of the week, and three times on Sundays. She dragged me along too, and once she even made me play the organ. She was so happy that everyone thought me brilliant.' He laughed. 'Can you imagine me playing the organ in church?'

'Actually, I can.' Honey smiled. 'Those are the memories to hold on to, Ashley, the good ones. In the end they're all that matter.'

He nodded. Then looked at her, his eyes soft with pain and need. 'I love you, Hon-Hon.'

Her breath caught in her throat and she stilled herself to hold it longer. Ashley's words released so much serotonin in her system she thought she would cry and she didn't want to, not now.

Ashley lowered his head to her stomach and started kissing the bump, gentle pecks as his hand stroked where his lips placed the kisses. 'Forgive your daddy for crying all over you,' he spoke gently to Honey's bump. 'Forgive me, okay?'

She dared to release her breath before her lungs could explode, and at that moment his head was once more level with hers, and his lips were coming for her lips, and she wanted this more than anything in the world. She ached with the want for him. Ashley was gentle; Honey was passion fuelled and shameless about what she wanted to do to him, and it was she who sat astride him and rode him and her into oblivion, right there on the living room floor.

After their love was spent, he continued kissing her bump.

Ashley spoke softly. 'Move in with me, Hon-Hon. I'll show you what I have to offer. Let me take care of my baby, please. We can turn the spare room into a nursery or some-thing, you can redecorate if you like, add your female energy.'

Honey was stunned. Something like this was what she had wanted, but she hadn't seen it coming and honestly didn't know what to say. There was the matter of Kevin to consider, and the fact that Ashley had just lost his mother, he was trau-matised. And what about his feelings for Bethany? She dared not take this seriously.

'Let's wait till the baby's born and see how things go,' she kissed his lips, savouring the feel.

'You love me?' he asked, and her heart flipped.

'As much as you love me,' she murmured.

'That much, huh? I wish I could be sure.'

Me too, she thought.

Twenty-Six

November 2016

Ashley arranged his mother's simple funeral with assistance from Dame and Auntie Dawn. She wanted to be cremated, her last wish in her will written the day after his father's departure from their lives. Marley hadn't said much since their mother's suicide, and it was so hard to read her. She showed no sadness and carried on as though everything was normal. Ashley dared not approach her, too filled with the knowledge that she did not know about her true parentage. Their aunt brought all that to an end the evening they sat down to dinner in her little flat.

'We know that only God knows why people do what they do. We know this is no-one's fault. Dee just wanted what she wanted. She's always been like that. And when she made up her mind to live in crazy land, it's because that's the only place she could forgive herself.'

Marley hadn't taken much notice and continued eating, but it suddenly surfaced in Ashley that his aunt must know more than she'd ever said.

'What does she need to forgive herself for, Auntie Dawn?' Ashley asked.

Auntie Dawn gave herself away by glancing briefly at Marley, but keeping her lips tightly pursed before returning her eyes to her plate and getting engrossed in the eating process.

'There are things that are better left unsaid,' she said simply.

'And unknown, by the looks of things,' Ashley said grimly, he too glancing briefly at Marley, who remained unconcerned about their conversation.

It was a Godsend when the doorbell rang and it was one of Marley's friends. It wasn't long before her music and girlish laughter could be heard through the closed door.

'Nate told me, Auntie Dawn.'

'Told you what?'

'About Marley. That Marley isn't Dad's child,' he whispered.

Auntie Dawn shook her head disappointingly. 'Nate shouldn't have told you. That was your mother's wish, that no-one should ever know, and your father accepted that.'

'So, it's true? Then who is Marley's father? She might need to know this one day.'

'No one knows, not even your moms. Dee was beautiful Ash, and it gave her a big head. She got lost in men's adulation.'

Try as he might, he couldn't remember. He didn't see any strange men in his home and said as much.

'You were at school, Ashley. She was very careful, she loved you so much.'

'But she loved Dad, so why was she doing this?'

'Your parents lived in the same house but, for months at a time, lived very separate lives. You were so young it all seemed normal to you. Dee gave as good as she got, and I often warned her it would lead her to hell. When she got pregnant, she never thought Elliott would ever leave her. You see, he worshipped her despite his affairs, but your father is a hypocrite. He always said a girl couldn't do what a guy does and still be called a lady.'

Ashley stood up angrily. This was too much. He gripped the table, moving his plate out of the way. He walked to the front door, not wanting to hear another word against his beloved mother, who had still to be laid to rest.

'I'm burying Moms tomorrow, tell Marley I'll see her there.' He left immediately, despite the call-back from his aunt. He phoned Honey. His call went to answer phone but he left no message.

The day of his mother's funeral was overcast, the skies as lifeless and motionless as her body, dressed in her favourite blue dress and very best church hat. Her face was made up and peaceful, with no sign of the trauma her death by hanging must have caused. He checked his watch and started feeling anxious that Honey hadn't arrived yet. She had promised to come.

He sensed, rather than saw, someone standing beside him. It was Marley. She had at least dressed in blue as he had requested of all family and friends attending the funeral. She glanced in the open casket briefly, her face relaxed, almost happy if he were honest.

'Marley, please just respect this day, okay?' His voice trembled with threatening tears and Marley's face softened with concern and apology.

'Sorry, Ash. I don't want to hurt you, but she was never a mother to me. She hated me, and you know it. She would cringe anytime she saw me, but you always forced me to see her.' She glanced once again in the casket. 'Not any more. I'm sorry for you that she's dead, and died in that way, but I'm not sorry.'

Ashley released his breath slowly. 'I'm sorry she made you feel that way and that I couldn't change things for you and Moms. I'm sorry, baby girl.'

Marley hugged her brother, resting her head against his chest. 'It's not your fault, Ash. I'm not damaged by it, honest. You're the best moms and dad I've ever had. I've only ever had you and course Auntie Dawn. I can't miss what I've never had.'

Dame arrived in a blue shirt and sky-blue tailored suit, slim fitting and hugging his slender form. His face was sombre and anxious.

'S'up' Ash,' he said with a cough. 'I'm here for you, okay? And you, Marley,' he hugged her briefly.

'Thanks, Dame,' Marley smiled brightly. 'I'll go see where Auntie Dawn is.'

'Honey called the studio because she can't get through to you.'

'My phone's been off—'

'Yes, we understand. She's in hospital—'

'What!'

'Calm down, she was having her regular antenatal. Her blood pressure was a little high so they kept her for the day, but she'll be home this evening. She can't attend, but she sends her love.'

Throughout the funeral service, Ashley kept wondering if Kevin was with Honey at the hospital, which only increased his misery. He was happy for the turn out though. There were so many people, many he didn't know. Whenever he saw any men around his mother's age he didn't know or recognise, he would glance for Marley's features on their faces and frustrate himself when nothing showed. The fact of the matter was, Marley looked like her mother. After the church service, he couldn't bring himself to attend the crematorium and it actually saddened him that Marley wanted to. She didn't want to return to the church hall to welcome everyone with hot soup and soft baked bread after the bleakness of the grave yard. He could tell she wanted to witness their mother being cremated to ensure she was really gone and, sadder than that, he couldn't blame her.

Twenty-Seven

21st December 2016

'Hi Ash, it's me, Fatty. Hon's water broke and we're in the hospital now.'

Ashley felt alarmed. 'That's early, isn't it? I mean she's not due for four days.'

'Well, your unpredictable child has decided to come early, dah. Where are you? Just get here as soon as you can, Hon's calling for you. Are you coming?' Fatty sounded doubtful.

'I'm on my way.' He grabbed his jacket and put it on at speed.

Marla came into her living room with a spreadsheet in her hand she had just taken from the printer. She had been going over the monthly accounts with Ashley and it was near to completion. 'Ash, what is it?'

'My baby's on the way.' He hurried to the door.

Marla couldn't hide the disappointment. 'Congratulations.'

He grabbed his coat and was out the door without another word. Checking his phone, he saw three missed calls from Honey hours earlier. *Shit.*

Natasha was already by her daughter's side, holding her hand and mopping her brow. She threw a look of indifference as Ashley entered the ward, gowned and looking terrified. Fatty was on the other side of Honey and she beckoned to Ashley to replace her. He approached gingerly. Honey looked so vulnerable that all he wanted to do was hold her close.

'Hon-Hon, this is it,' he gave a small smile. 'You're gonna be a Mama.' He didn't know where that optimistic, jovial voice came from.

'It's so painful... I never thought it would be this baaaaaad,' she screamed as another contraction came.

The midwife examined her. 'Right. Now the hard work begins. It's time to push as hard as you can.'

'Hard work begins?' Honey looked in hopeless disbelief at the smiling face of the midwife. 'Hard work begins? What the fuck have I been going through the past nine hours? I can't,' she screamed. The bare white walls of the delivery room terrified her. Why the hell couldn't they put up wallpaper or something? The blinding lights beaming down on her were too intrusive. It magnified the indescribable pain that took her to the tip of unconsciousness and back again.

'I'm not going to make it, it hurts too much!'

'Push, Honey!' the midwife urged.

'Can't you give her something for the pain?' Fatty queried.

The midwife looked calm and relaxed. 'Too late for that.'

'I'm pushing all I can,' she turned towards her mother. 'Tasha, it hurts.'

Her mother kissed her sweaty forehead. 'I know sweetie,

do as the midwife tells you and it'll be easier. Your baby wants to meet you.'

Honey felt heat like she'd ever felt before. Ashley squeezed her hand reassuringly but she withdrew as another contraction caused her to scream.

'Get it out!'

'Baby's head is coming, good girl,' the midwife cooed.

Finally, she pushed out her baby, exhausted and relieved, and the strangest thing happened. The bright lights were no longer intrusive. Instead they bathed her, and she suddenly felt the need to cry at the sight of the life she'd carried for nine months. Patches of maternal blood stood out on little legs and arms unfolding, and all she could see was a little face with closed, puffy eyes and thick black hair.

'It's a girl!' Fatty cried.

Then she heard her mother crying and felt the kisses on her face. The midwife placed the baby on top of her chest and she was almost afraid to touch her. She looked for Ashley.

'I told you it's a girl,' he smiled, leaning over and stroking the damp curls of the baby's head. 'A little girl,' he said, more to himself. A great flood ran through him. He felt protective towards this little thing. She was a lot smaller than Marley had been, Ashley noted, and wondered how anything so small would be able to survive. He had made this baby.

While the baby was being checked and Honey cleaned up, Ashley slipped outside in the chilled December evening air. He stood with his hands in his brown cashmere jacket pocket, his eyes focused on the huge tree in the forecourt of the hospital grounds. People were arriving with huge bunches of flowers, arms laden with parcels wrapped with pink or blue bows, and balloons that said 'boy' or 'girl'. He was a father, the one thing he never wanted to be. But that little bundle had caused a volcano of emotions to erupt within him.

'Hello daddy.' Ashley turned quickly to see Fatty in front of him.

He smiled, then turned away.

'Hon's asking for you, they're taking her and the baby down to the ward now.'

'I'm coming. Just needed a bit of air. What you poor women have to go through, huh!'

Fatty slipped her hand in his as they headed back inside. 'You're cold. Are you alright, Ash?'

'A little in shock. I just became a father to a little girl—I don't know, I feel even more protective than when Marley was born.'

'Don't break her heart,' Fatty pleaded.

'You talk as if I'm going to run out on her any minute.'

'Are you?' Fatty peered at him.

'I haven't felt this way about a woman in two years.'

'Yeah, I know. We're all on your side, hate what Beth did with that Bruce.'

'That's water under the bridge. Come on, I want to see my daughter again.'

When they arrived back and finally found Honey in a private room, Kevin was standing there in a pristine white jumper and black cut trousers. Natasha placed the baby in his arms, despite seeing the disapproval run across Ashley's face. Kevin cradled the baby, cooing, and Honey looked pleadingly at Ashley. He was mad, but fell into her pleading eyes. He stood still and watched the charade Natasha was encouraging with Kevin.

'She looks just like Honey did,' Natasha said to Kevin while stroking the baby's hand. 'You'd better get used to your turn changing nappies,' she gave a small laugh.

'She looks just like her father,' Honey said flatly, not willing to alienate Ashley in the way her mother was encouraging Kevin to do. 'Even down to the dimpled chin.'

Ashley gave her a grateful smile.

'No, she definitely looks like you did at birth,' Natasha insisted.

Ashley made his move then and gently removed his daughter from Kevin's arms. There was a moment of resistance as both men's eyes met, but then Kevin relaxed his grip and Ashley took his daughter and sat on the hospital bed beside Honey.

'I think she has your frown,' he smiled at Honey. 'Look, she's already frowning,' he laughed, Honey joining in.

'She's possibly frowning at what's ahead for her, father wise—'

'Tasha!' Honey glared.

Natasha was in her usual agitated, empowered state that automatically flowed whenever Ashley Elliott was around. 'Well, it's got to be said,' Natasha continued. 'He hasn't even asked you to marry him—'

'Mother, you need to stop this right now!' Honey snapped.

'Why can't you see, huh? Why can't you see he's not ready for a baby, for any life of responsibility? He owns a club! You have a good man here in Kevin, willing and ready to be a husband and a father,' Natasha placed a gentle hand on a smug Kevin's shoulder.

Fatty, sitting quietly in the corner all the time was brought to life by that smug look on Kevin's face. It wasn't anyone but Honey's decision who would make a good husband for her. Fatty wanted to say this but knew Natasha would alienate her for life, so instead she looked encouragingly at Honey to say something before Ashley did. *Too late.*

'I'm this little girl's daddy,' Ashley spoke towards Natasha and Kevin, standing side by side like members of a legion. 'She's your first grandchild but my child, my daughter, my baby... Natatrash.'

Natasha cringed as Kevin came to her rescue.

'Her name is Natasha, have some respect!'

Ashley glared at him, suddenly stalled by the touch of Honey's hand on his arm. He was still cradling his baby, this absolutely new wonder to his mind, and he didn't want to let any anger out in her soft, tiny presence.

Kevin looked sternly at Honey. 'I need to talk to you alone.' It sounded like a demand.

Natasha came in quickly. 'Of course you can, you deserve an explanation.'

'For what?' Ashley snapped.

Honey looked at Kevin. 'I don't think this is the place, but yes, let's talk. If you don't mind leaving for five minutes,' she pleadingly addressed all in the room.

Ashley placed his baby in the cot beside the bed, apprehensive of what Honey might want to say privately to Kevin. He didn't know how deep Honey's feelings went for Kevin, but she had slept with him, so for all Ashley knew he could be the loser.

When the room had emptied, Kevin stood, looking trapped and frustrated.

'What are you doing?' Honey asked.

'I should be asking you the same. I love you, why won't you let me prove how much?'

Honey viewed him kindly. 'Thank you, Kev.' She took a deep breath. 'I know you mean well and I appreciate it. I've thought seriously about your proposal. At one point I thought we, me, you and the baby, could make it. But now she's here and she's a real person, looking like her own daddy who wants to be a part of her life. I don't see how I can deny that.'

Kevin remained speechless for a full silent minute. 'I can accept he can be in the child's life, but what about your life? Are you telling me goodbye?'

Honey felt choked and unsure. She knew Kevin loved her and he would love her baby too, of that she was certain. But the simple fact was that she loved Ashley, and there was a part of her that wished she didn't, a part of her that feared her mother's prediction, that feared he still loved Bethany, but she loved him and when her tiny baby gave a contented breath in her arms, she knew what she had to do.

Love Again

'I'm sorry, Kev. You can see the position I'm in, and I'm still not sure I'm making the right decision for me, but I am for my daughter. She deserves to grow with her daddy.'

Kevin's smile was weak, lopsided and broken.

'I wish there was something I could do to change your mind, but I'm no fool. I can see my efforts would be wasted. You really love him, don't you? You always have. Every time you look at me, you're looking for him. I hope he turns out to be worthy of you, but I doubt it very much, and deep in your heart I think you know that too. Bye, Honey.'

Twenty-Eight

March 2017

Starr-Bright Marley Elliott was the name they settled on. Ashely surprised himself at how quickly he adjusted to fatherhood, how he enjoyed holding his daughter, bringing up her wind and changing her nappy. If it wasn't for Natasha, he would visit his new addition more regularly. She had his amber eyes, dimpled chin, nose and his mouth; only the soft, curly, downy hair belonged to Honey. Starr-Bright had a mixture of them both.

Ashley woke up and watched Honey from the chair in her bedroom he had fallen asleep in. She'd just finished breast-feeding Starr and had gently placed the baby upright on her shoulder whilst she rubbed her back. Ashley glanced at the clock on the wall: 2:45am. He yawned and Honey looked at him, smiling.

'Did we wake you?' she enquired, still rubbing her baby's back.

Ashley shook his head and sat beside her on the bed. Using a finger, he stroked the baby's dimpled chin, circling her ear.

The child stirred on her mother's shoulder.

'Let me hold her.' He held out his hands, taking the baby and placing her on his chest. She settled immediately and he placed a soft kiss on the top of her mass of black curls. He inhaled her. 'I kind of love this baby smell... I can't remember Marley smelling this good, but then I was only ten when she was born and all she did was eat, throw up, cry and shit.'

Honey laughed and placed her head on her pillow. 'She's getting better at sleeping longer hours. I can't wait for her to sleep through and come off the breast. I think I'll breast feed her up to six months—'

'I hear a year is better. Gives them less allergies as they grow.'

She giggled. 'What do you know about—'

'There's no excuse not to know about everything, not with the internet. Let's put Starr down to sleep... then let me put you to sleep,' his voice was low and seductive.

Honey and Ashley lay on their sides facing each other after an hour of slow, sensuous love making. They were both wet with each other's sweat, both fired up by each other's touch and feel. Ashley wrapped a strand of her hair around his finger. 'You amaze me... I can't get enough of you.'

'I'm going to love you forever.' she told him.

'You promise? Move in with me. I meant it when I asked you before,' he said. He didn't like the way his daughter, even though she was only three months old, reacted with more enthusiasm at seeing Natasha than him. Just last week, when he'd gone to collect Honey and Starr to spend the weekend with him, he'd picked up his baby and she'd screwed up her little face into an angry ball before letting out a scream, that if you didn't know any better, you'd think he'd pinched her. Starr only shut up on that occasion when Natasha had swiftly removed her from his arms. Honey curled herself around him, pulling him in with her leg. 'You really mean it, Ashley?'

'Yes, I do... marry me.'

'Give me five good reasons.'

He continued playing with the strand of her hair around his finger. 'You're something else. Okay, let me see. Number one, I love you. Two, I want to spend forever with you. Three, you're a good moms. I want you to be the mother of all my children. Four, I'm good in bed—aha, don't interrupt me, and five, I'll never leave you. I want our daughter to grow with us. I want to wake up and I want to go to sleep with you beside me. I want to come home to you and Starr. I mean it, and I'll prove it.'

Epilogue

April 2017

The day finally arrived. 21st April: Fatty and Fredrick's wedding day. The spring sun was already bright and low in the sky, more blue than white; a good sign for the beginning of two lives together, Honey thought as she and Starr got in the car. She was meeting Fatty at the hotel to help dress her for her special day. Ashley had worked late at the club and was joining them later.

Fatty's and Freddy's day was titled 'My Big Fat Caribbean-Brazilian Wedding,' and Freddy had spared no expense in giving Fatty the wedding she had dreamt about. Fatty was a bag of nerves as the professional makeup artist worked on her face. She watched her reflection in the mirror being transformed into the princess from her dreams. Honey helped her into her Vera Wang cream wedding creation, and she slipped her feet into elegant slender six-inch heeled, cream and gold Jimmy Choo sandals. Finally, Honey placed the tiara on her carefully styled hair. The friends stood side by side looking at each other in the mirror.

'You look magnificent, Fatty, I'm so happy for you. I wish Za was here to see you. We got to send her some videos and pictures. I hope they don't marry her off over there.'

'She told the British High Commission before she left.' Fatty chuckled. 'She wasn't taking any chances. She did say she would be back for the wedding, but you know Za, probably found some disco in the desert.'

Honey laughed at the thought. 'That would be Za.'

Fatty took a deep breath. 'I owe this happiness to you, Hon. If you hadn't told me about Freddy's feelings for me, I'd most probably be stuck with—'

'No, you wouldn't. You would've eventually found love.'

'I never thought I would ever see this day,' Fatty stared unblinkingly at her reflection. 'I really never, ever thought I would be this happy, Hon. There is a God.' She put her hands together in prayer.

Honey turned and adjusted the tiara on Fatty's head. 'You deserve the best, Fats, and I just know once you're settled and relaxed, you'll be able to have your baby.'

Fatty's face softened. 'I want to share something with you. You're the only one I tell absolutely everything that means anything. You're my heart-beat, Hon.'

'And you're mine, Fats. Friends for life.'

'Freddy and I have decided if I don't get pregnant within two years, then we'll try IVF a maximum of two times. If that fails, we'll adopt from West Africa, Ghana—Angelina and Madonna did it, Vanesse Derby can do it too.'

Honey looked astonished, then hugged her friend carefully,

not wanting to disturb her wedding dress. 'You and Freddy will have your baby, I just know it. But you listen to me now: today's your day. Go out there and get married to your ride or die. After the honeymoon we can book you some spa-relaxing time and a therapist to help you to unblock and release. Don't think about making babies right now—just enjoy the ride.'

Fatty laughed. 'Thanks, Hon. The thing I most want in this world is to share a child with Freddy.'

'You'll have your baby. You deserve it, Fats.'

'I think I believe you. Come, let's get downstairs before your daughter starts yelling for you.'

Ashley was as good as his word. When the bride and chief bridesmaid came downstairs, he was dressed in a light royal blue suit with a stark white shirt, which was unbuttoned at the neck, and his hair held back in a ponytail. He was holding Starr and talking to the other bridesmaids. His eyes held Honey as she walked towards him and he couldn't help thinking how beautiful she looked. She could've easily been the bride. Without thinking, he kissed her.

'You look delicious,' he smiled. 'And Fatty, wow! Look at you! Happiness suits you.'

'Thanks, Ash.'

'You look fucking gorge, Fats.' Fatty turned swiftly, both her and Honey squealing in unison.

'Za! When did you get back? Girl, I swear they married you off to some cousin in Somalia.'

Zhara, dressed in a fitted silver catsuit, accessorised with sparkling hooped earrings, her long hair squeezed in a tight bun, was careful as she placed her cheek to Fatty's, then Honey's.

'I wasn't going to miss my bestie's wedding for nothing. OMG, I missed you guys. But guess what?' she whispered. 'I met some-one at the airport, well, he's a pilot and I want you guys to—'

Honey stepped in, laughing. 'Za, it's about Fatty today. But we'll hear about your pilot after the wedding.'

'Fucking hell, Za, I want to hear all about it before the end of the night, trust me. But now, let's go get me the love of my life.'

Fatty had asked Dame to give her away and he'd jumped at the chance. All through the ceremony, Fatty kept thinking she would wake up and it would all have been a dream, so when the priest finally pronounced them man and wife, she breathed a sigh of relief and fell against Fredrick.

They danced to Al Green's *Lets Stay Together*. She rested her head on his shoulders, feeling more happiness than she could stand. She closed her eyes. She was a married woman. A man loved her enough to make her his wife.

Ashley pulled Honey to dance. 'Where's Starr?'

'Tasha has her out in the small hall.'

'Your old manager called just before I left the house. Says she wants to talk to you,' he whispered in her ear. 'It sounds like they want you back.'

'I'll only consider going back as a consultant, and part time. I want Starr to have me around until she starts school.'

Ashley pulled her in closer. 'Thank you, for being a super

261

moms to our daughter.'

'Honey,' Natasha halted their dance. 'Hi Ashley,' she said, with mild courtesy to him.

'Starr has a dirty nappy. Don't worry, the hotel staff has given me a room to change her—doesn't Vanesse look stunning, absolutely stunning? I told her so. Marriage gives a woman security and shows that a man is serious.' Natasha let her eyes linger on Ashley longer than was necessary, before walking off with Starr.

Honey fell back into Ashley's arms and continued dancing. 'You know she was hinting to you about marriage.'

'Yeah, I figured,' he chuckled. 'Let's throw a big party and tell her in front of all her friends that I'm going to officially be her son-in-law.'

Honey kissed him. 'You know, I think she'll be relieved. She wants her friends to see I wasn't left a single mother. Plus, she's impressed with the size of your bank account, if nothing else.'

'We'll work on her. She'll eventually see me as the asset that I am for her daughter. I'm a parent of a daughter now, so I know what all parents of girls want—the best for their princess,' he stroked her cheek. 'For them to find the right love, that loves them back. I can't stand the thought of any man hurting my Starr. We should get into the arranged marriage culture, find her a husband ourselves. I finally get Tasha.'

Honey laughed. 'She'll be so happy to hear that. And you actually called her by her correct name!'

'If she's going to be my mother-in-law, it's only fair I make an effort... and right at this moment, I'm so happy you love me, there would be no limits to my efforts. I love you Honey Fontaine, soon to be Honey Elliott. I can't wait.'

'Me too. Only I was thinking you should take my surname, there being no limits to your efforts.'

'Why not? Sounds good. Ashley Fontaine-Elliott, wow, I can see Tasha's face now.'

Acknowledgements

Big thanks to my publisher, the Jacaranda 'Dream Team', my editor, Cherise Lopes-Baker, a great pair of listening ears...

To the Women who saved me: Sharon Tucker, Empress Makeda, Tafia Blair, Marcia Gordon, Kandake Makonnen, Angela Stewart, Lucille Bertolaso-Scarlett, LaKeisha Smith, Mawah Al-Gouri, Hayley Garner-Spencer, Debrina Chambers, Mairaz El-Fatih, Shawn Martin, Alinthia Fennel.